Secrets, Suspicions, and Silence

THE SECOND BOOK IN THE MISADVENTURE AND MYSTERY SERIES

By Travis Cramer

Edited by Violet Cramer

Secrets, Suspicions, and Silence

Misadventure and Mystery, Volume 2

Travis Cramer

Published by Travis Cramer, 2024.

SECRETS, SUSPICIONS, AND SILENCE

First edition. July 10, 2024.

Copyright © 2024 Travis Cramer.

ISBN: 979-8227290229

Written by Travis Cramer.

Table of Contents

Chapter 1

"Erica, for the last time, I'm not doing it!" Scott and Erica were sitting in Scott's living room and Erica was trying to convince Scott to take fencing lessons with her.

"Why not? It'll be fun!" Erica said, tossing a magazine at Scott. "Look at these pictures. Doesn't this look thrilling?" Scott thumbed through the magazine.

"Yeah, thrilling," Scott muttered. "If you like getting smacked in the face by a sword." He flipped to a page in the magazine of a fencer swinging a foil at another fencer's face and showed it to Erica. "Look at this! I like my face, thanks."

"You'll be wearing eye protection. And you're not using swords, you're using foils. They're super light and barely hurt at all. Come on, please!" Erica begged. "You'll love it."

Scott sighed. "Sports aren't really my thing," he said. "I prefer computers. There's much less danger in that." He got up from his chair and walked over to the fridge. "Want some fruit?" he asked Erica, pulling an apple from the fruit drawer.

Erica shook her head. "I'm good. And fencing is hardly a sport. It's an art, and an essential self-defense skill."

Scott rolled his eyes. "Yeah, because I'm always going to be carrying around a sword everywhere I go. I think karate would be more helpful. Why don't you ask Adrian or Phoebe to take lessons with you?"

"It's a foil, not a sword, and I already asked Adrian. He said his driving lessons were during the fencing lesson's times." Erica said.

Adrian was 16 and had just gotten his learner's permit a few days ago. He was taking the driving lessons the school provided and was spending most of his time practicing with his dad.

"And Phoebe?" Scott asked.

Erica looked at him with a look that meant "You're joking, right?"

"Okay, you're right. Phoebe would never even think about something like that," Scott said, thinking about all the times Phoebe had complained about any form of physical exercise. According to her, there was no need to strain her body when she could strain her mind and gain far more benefits.

"Exactly. So, you're my only other option."

Scott picked up the magazine again and looked at it. "Why do you want someone else to join anyway? You've never asked us to play any other sports you play. Why this one?"

"Well, I need a partner that I can practice with between lessons. After all, that's the only way to learn something."

"How about Teddy or Lucy?" Scott suggested. "Teddy likes sports, doesn't he?" Teddy and Lucy were Erica's younger twin sisters.

Erica sighed. "Lucy is more of a bookworm than Phoebe. As for Teddy, well, you've never had a younger sibling, but something you should know about them is that if you don't let them beat you in something, they'll have a tantrum and go complain to your parents. Then you'll get in trouble, and you'll have to let them win from then on."

Scott chuckled. "Sounds fun." He took a bite of his apple. "I'll talk to my parents about learning fencing. They've been nagging me to do some afterschool activities, anyway."

"Awesome!" Erica said. "The first lesson starts in a week and a half." She grabbed her magazine off the table and shoved it in her backpack. "Speaking of the twins, I should get home to check on them before they kill each other. See you at school tomorrow."

"Yep, see you," Scott said, tossing his apple core in the trash. Erica grabbed her backpack, and Scott absentmindedly watched her leave.

Scott was home alone, since Greg had left for college after summer break ended. He only came home on holidays and Scott would never be willing to admit it, but he did miss him occasionally.

Scott was busy as well, though. Since he was now a sophomore in high school, along with Erica and Phoebe, he had more homework than last year. Which is another reason he wasn't too keen on joining Erica in learning fencing.

Of course, Phoebe should have been a freshman instead of a sophomore, but she had decided to skip the final grade of middle school, since she was practically college level in some subjects, and she figured that it would be a waste of time to finish middle school, and instead went straight to high school.

Scott sighed and flipped open his laptop. His unfinished report started back at him, and he closed the file. It was Monday, and the report was due on Friday, so he had a few days, but Scott was quite the procrastinator and probably wouldn't finish the report until the last minute.

Bored, Scott checked his phone for any messages from his parents. They were both working at the store, and Scott usually didn't see them until a while after he had gotten home from school. Instead of a message from his parents, he found a text from Adrian. It read:

"Hey, can u help me fix my bike?"

Scott was good at fixing bikes, since it felt like his was broken every other day. Adrian and Erica would often ask Scott for help in fixing their bikes when they had problems.

"Sure, can u bring it over?" Scott asked. He put his phone down, but it vibrated shortly after he had sent the text. It was another text from Adrian. "Yep, I'll be over in about 20 min."

Scott sent a thumbs-up emoji, and went back to blankly staring at his essay, wondering what to write. After about 5 minutes of staring and thinking, he finally decided that he'd work on his report tomorrow.

15 minutes later, the doorbell rang. It was Adrian, standing there with his bike. Scott greeted him and said "Hey Adrian, what's up with your bike?"

"The brakes aren't working very well," said Adrian. "I hit the lever, but it takes a while to stop."

"I'll see what I can do," Scott said. He walked over to Adrian's bike and looked at the brakes. "Well, the problem is that the brake pads are misaligned," he said. "I'll see if I can fix it."

Scott walked over to his shed and grabbed a screwdriver and a pair of pliers. "So, how are driving lessons going?" he asked Adrian, while unscrewing the brake pad. "Think you'll get your license before then end of school?"

"I don't know," said Adrian. "It's a lot harder than I was expecting, so it might take me a while."

Scott stuck the screwdriver in the ground and picked up the pliers. "Yeah, Greg taught me how to drive last summer. The hardest part for me was knowing how soon to hit the brakes."

"Wait, you know how to drive?" Adrian asked. "You're not even 16 yet."

"Well, I don't have a license, so I can't legally drive, but technically speaking, I do know how to drive," Scott answered, twisting the brake pad back into place. "I'll have to wait until I'm 16."

"So, if you know how to drive, can you help me learn?" Adrian asked.

"Legally, no," said Scott. "I think you need to have someone over 18 with a driver's license in the car with you, if you're driving."

"Well, you wouldn't be driving with me," said Adrian. "Maybe you could just give me some tips and advice."

Scott screwed the brake pad back on and laughed. "I doubt I'm the best person to ask for driving advice. I only know the basics of driving. You'd be better off asking your parents to help you."

"Well, I did, but they're always so busy. My dad only has about an hour everyday to help me, and my mom isn't very good at teaching."

"Well, I can try to help you," Scott said, pressing the brake pedal. He wheeled the bike over to Scott. "All good."

Adrian took the bike from Scott. "Thanks a lot. And I really would appreciate it a lot if you helped me learn to drive."

Scott picked his tools off the ground and started towards the shed. "All right, I'll help you out after school tomorrow," he said. "Just take everything I say with a grain of salt."

Adrian chuckled. "I always do," he said, before biking off. "See you tomorrow!" he called to Scott. Scott chucked his tools back into the shed and went back inside.

Chapter II

The next day at school, Scott was sitting with Adrian and Phoebe in the cafeteria, but strangely, Erica didn't seem to be joining them.

"Have you seen Erica lately?" Adrian asked. "I didn't see her at all today."

"No, now that you mention it, I haven't seen her either," said Phoebe. "Scott, did you see her?"

Scott shook his head. "No, I figured that she was probably sick or something. Which is strange considering that I just saw her yesterday. She was asking me to join her in taking fencing lessons."

Phoebe shrugged. "Maybe she had somewhere else to go. Like a doctor's appointment or a sports try-out."

Adrian chuckled. "Well, it wouldn't be the first time that she skipped school to go join a new sports team. It's practically a regular thing."

"Yeah, I guess," said Scott. "She didn't say anything about a sports team, though. Oh well, I guess we can visit her after school, and ask her why she wasn't here today."

Phoebe and Adrian nodded in agreement. "Yeah, I was going to ask her if she could help Katie with soccer practice."

Katie was Adrian's younger sister, and unlike Adrian, she enjoyed playing sports. Unfortunately for Adrian, he wasn't very good at sports, so he couldn't really help Katie practice much.

Scott looked at the food on the tray sitting on the table. "I really need to start bringing my own lunch," he said. "The food here gets worse every year."

Phoebe gestured to her salad. "You should have done that years ago, like me. I would never eat school food. Who knows what they put in it?"

Adrian rolled his eyes. "You guys are too picky. I think the food tastes great."

"Yeah, but you think all food tastes great, even if it literally tastes like dirt," said Scott.

Adrian shrugged. "Like I said, you guys are too picky. As long as it's not poisonous, I'll be happy to eat it."

"Great, you can eat my chili," said Scott, dumping the pile of gooey chili and beans onto Adrian's tray. "Enjoy."

"Jokes on you, the chili is the best part of the school lunch," said Adrian.

Scott shook his head and said "Whatever. Glad somebody here likes it."

Phoebe put her fork down and looked at Adrian. "You know, for someone who grows their own food, I would have expected you to be choosier about what you eat."

Adrian shrugged again. "I don't grow food to stay healthy. I grow it because it's fun, and it's cheaper than buying groceries. Plus, my parents really like my garden."

"I'll bet they do," said Scott with his mouth full. "My parents are always complaining about how much I eat."

Phoebe winced. "Don't talk with your mouth full," she said. "It's gross."

Scott raised his eyebrows, something he had learned from Greg. "We only have 30 minutes for lunch. That means I have to cram in all my eating and talking in only half an hour. It's good to multitask."

Adrian cracked up, while Phoebe shook her head saying, "You're hopeless."

"Say, did you hear about Old Man McGinnis?" Adrian asked.

"What? Did his car get stolen again?" asked Scott. A few months ago, McGinnis' car had been stolen which eventually led to a string of car thefts. The four of them had helped the police catch the criminals and put them behind bars. Impressed with their work, the police chief had given them special badges making them honorary detectives.

"No, but his house was robbed," Adrian said. "I don't know when, but it was sometime yesterday."

"Wow, poor guy. He keeps getting targeted by criminals," said Phoebe. "Did he have cameras?"

"Nope. You'd think he would have learned from last time, but I guess not," said Adrian.

"What was taken?" asked Scott.

Adrian shrugged. "I don't know. I just heard it from our neighbor. He mentioned to us and warned us to be careful."

The three of them finished eating and discussing table manners and the robbery and headed back off to class after the bell rang.

After school, Scott, Adrian, and Phoebe met up in the parking lot outside the gym. They each grabbed their bikes, and headed off to Erica's house to ask her where she was. When they got here, Adrian knocked on the door and Erica's mom answered.

"Hi kids. How can I help you?" she asked.

"Hi Mrs. Feldman," Adrian said. "Is Erica home?"

Erica's mom looked confused. "No...I figured she would be with you. She hasn't come home from school yet."

Now Adrian looked confused. "School? We didn't see her at school at all; we figured that she wasn't feeling well, or that she had somewhere else to go."

"What? No, are you sure?" asked Erica's mom. "She definitely went to school today. I made her breakfast and watched her leave the house. She must have been there."

Adrian looked at Scott and Phoebe. "It's possible," said Adrian. "But I didn't see her in any of our classes, and she didn't sit with us at lunch."

"Well, she has been very busy lately," Erica's mom replied. "I can't think why she would miss her classes, though. Are you sure you didn't see her at all?"

They all shook their heads. "Normally we see her at lunch, since we all sit at the same table, but she wasn't there today," said Scott.

"That's very odd," Erica's mom said. "I'm sure that she was probably just busy during lunch, probably with sports or something and might have missed lunch. It's possible that you just didn't see her in classes."

Adrian shrugged. "It's possible, I guess," he said, not sounding convinced. "Can you just tell Erica to call us when she gets home?"

"Yes, we tried calling her cell phone after school, but she didn't answer," Phoebe said.

"Oh, of course," Erica's mom replied. "I'll let her know that you three dropped by."

Adrian, Scott, and Phoebe all said thanks and waved goodbye to Erica's mom and hopped back on their bikes. As they were biking down the road, Scott said "I'm pretty sure I didn't see Erica at school. In fact, I'm almost positive. I would have at least seen her in P.E. if not any of the other classes."

Phoebe shrugged. "Maybe she's playing hooky. Or maybe she just something else to do."

"Hooky?" asked Scott. "Erica? I doubt it. And why would she have something to do and not tell her parents about it."

Phoebe shrugged again. "It's not really our business. If Erica has something important to do, there's probably a reason that she didn't tell us."

Adrian scrunched his eyebrows. "I know, but she's our friend. What if something happened to her?"

"Adrian's right," said Scott. "We should go back to school and see if anyone saw her at school."

Phoebe sighed. "But why? Logic dictates that the safest and most sensible thing to do would be to go home, finish our homework, and wait for Erica to call us."

"Well, sometimes you have to think outside the box," Scott said, turning his bike around and pedaling back towards school with Adrian right behind him.

"No, that's not-" Phoebe groaned and turned her bike around to follow Scott and Adrian. "This is a hopeless endeavor," she called to Scott. "There's nothing that we need to do."

"Maybe not, but at least we can figure out where she went," Scott called over her shoulder.

Annoyed, Phoebe followed Scott and Adrian back to the school. They parked their bikes in the parking lot and walked over to the school. There were a couple people playing basketball on the courts, and another few people hanging out in the parking lot, but besides that, the school was mostly empty.

"See, I told you this was pointless," Phoebe said. "There's nobody here."

"Not necessarily," said Adrian, walking towards the entrance. "Principal Peterson is probably still here."

Shaking her head and still annoyed, Phoebe followed Adrian and Scott into the school. They walked down the empty hallways until the came to the principal's office. Scott knocked on the door, and the principal answered.

"Scott? Adrian, Phoebe? What can I do for you?" he asked. "Shouldn't you be home by now?"

"Well, normally, yes," said Adrian, "But we were wondering if you saw Erica at school at all today."

Principal Peterson scratched his head. "No, I don't believe so," he said. "I don't recall her having a note from her parents either, so I'll have to talk to her tomorrow." He looked at Scott, Adrian, and Phoebe. "Do you know where she went?"

Scott shook his head. "That's why we were asking you. We didn't see her at school all day, and she hasn't come home yet."

Principal Peterson looked concerned. "I certainly didn't see her in any of the classes, and I don't recall seeing her come in when the bell rang."

Scott, Adrian, and Phoebe all looked at each other. "You're sure you didn't see her at all?" Adrian asked. The principal nodded. "Positive," he said.

"Okay, thanks Principal," said Phoebe. "I'm sure that she had something else to do and forgot to let us know."

"No doubt," Principal Peterson said. "However, when you see her, just tell her that I'd like a word or two with her before school tomorrow."

"Will do," said Phoebe, leaving the office and practically dragging Scott and Adrian out with him.

Once they were outside the office, Adrian asked "What the heck was that about? Why'd you leave in such a hurry."

"Look, if Principal Peterson didn't see Erica at school, and her mom says that she isn't home, that means she's probably playing hooky, and I don't want to get involved with that," said Phoebe. "If she wants to skip school, that's her choice, but I want no part in it."

Phoebe marched off away from Scott and Adrian and grabbed her bike. She pedaled away from the school, and didn't look back at Scott or Adrian.

Adrian scratched his forehead. "What was that about?" he asked Scott.

Scott shrugged. "No idea. She's probably right, though. If Erica wasn't at school today, she was probably skipping it on purpose."

"Yeah, but why?" Adrian asked. "That's not like Erica. You, I can see skipping school, but not Erica."

"Me? How can you see me skipping school? I've rarely even missed a class," Scott said indignantly.

"That's besides the point, okay," said Adrian. "It's just...I don't know." Adrian stopped talking for a second and looked away. "We should probably get home," he said.

"I guess so," Scott said. "Let me know if you hear from Erica." Scott and Adrian walked back towards their bikes and headed home after saying goodbye to each other.

The rest of the day was uneventful for all three of them. They finished up their homework and did their daily chores. It wasn't until around an hour before nightfall that Adrian texted Scott and asked "Hey, did u hear from Erica yet. I didn't get any calls or texts."

Scott grabbed his phone and was about to reply to Adrian text, when he changed his mind and dialed Erica's number. The call went straight to voicemail without even ringing once. He tried again, but got the same result. He tried again, and again, and again, but each time the call went right to voicemail.

Instead of calling again, Scott texted Adrian and said "Nothing from Erica. I tried calling her, but there was no response. Can you meet up with me and Phoebe at my house?"

Meanwhile, Adrian was busy watering his plants and he was lost in thought. He was thinking about Erica and where she could be. He didn't realize how lost in thought he was until his phone vibrated and he snapped back to reality and noticed that he had practically flooded his pepper seedlings.

Adrian put the watering can down and drained the water from the plant before checking his phone. It was just a news alert, but it made Adrian realize how concerned he was about Erica. Normally nothing could distract him from his plants, but here he was, absentmindedly overwatering his seedlings.

Adrian's dad was still at work and he normally didn't come home until 7PM and Adrian's mom had gone out to the store to grab some groceries. Which meant that he was home alone with-

"Adrian, come here. I need your help!" Katie called out from the living room for the eighth time today.

Adrian sighed. Katie really was a pain in the butt sometimes, but since his parents weren't home, it was his job to watch Katie. And ever since she had turned 7, she had made it her goal to annoy the living daylights out of Adrian. At least it felt like that to Adrian.

"Adrian! Where are you!?" Katie called again.

Adrian put his phone back in his pocket and called "I'm coming! Give me a minute." He left his greenhouse after killing a beetle that had gotten in somehow and walked towards the living room.

He found Katie sitting at the table, holding a pencil and writing on a piece of paper.

"What's the matter, Katie?" Adrian asked. "What do you need me for?"

Katie held up the paper she was writing on. It was her math homework and she had only gotten through the first problem.

"Can you help me with my homework?" Katie asked.

Mentally, Adrian sighed again. To Katie, he said "Of course, what problem do you need help with?"

"All of them!" Katie said, enthusiastically.

This time, Adrian sighed aloud. Helping Katie basically just meant giving her the answer. He was about to sit next to her and prepare for a half hour of torture when his phone went off. It was Scott's text asking them to meet and Adrian couldn't be happier to see that text. Anything to help him get away from tutoring Katie.

"Well, my parents aren't home right now, so I can't leave Katie alone, but we can meet in my house instead," he texted.

Scott responded right away and said "That works. I'll be there in a bit."

Over at Phoebe's house, things were a bit different. She was completely immersed in the book that she had been reading for the past 2 hours. She often got caught up in a book, and sometimes even forgot to eat since she was so focused on her book.

She was home alone, since her parents were at work and she was an only child, so when she started reading a book, there was almost nothing to distract her. Almost nothing, except for her phone.

Phoebe had been obsessively checking her phone every time it went off in hopes of finding the results of the contest she had entered. Her science project for the school fair had won 1st place, like always, but she had decided to expand and enter her project in a statewide competition.

Phoebe's phone went off, and like always, she immediately put her book down and grabbed her phone. She checked her notifications, but it was just a text from Adrian. It said, "Hey, have u heard from Erica at all?"

Disappointed, Phoebe ignored the text and went back to reading her book. She really didn't want to think about Erica. In her eyes, if Erica wanted to play hooky and do whatever she was doing, that was her problem.

Phoebe was a stickler for all things related to school. In her opinion, school was one of the most important things for anyone. She looked down on anyone who skipped school for any reason.

Nevertheless, despite her views, Phoebe couldn't deny that she was at least a little concerned for Erica. After all, what Adrian had said was true. It really wasn't like Erica to skip school. Frustrated, Phoebe tried to focus on her book, but no matter how hard she tried, she simply couldn't concentrate anymore.

Sighing, Phoebe stuck a bookmark in book and tossed it on her bed. Knowing she probably wasn't going to be able to get anymore reading today, she picked her phone up again and opened her texts. She responded to Adrian's and text and said "No, I haven't. I'm sure she'll be home soon."

Phoebe stood up and walked to the kitchen. Before she could get something out of the fridge her phone went off again. This time, it was a text from Adrian asking if she could meet him and Scott at his house.

Phoebe closed the fridge and asked Adrian what he wanted to meet for. Adrian responded quickly and said that he just wanted to see if they could figure out where Erica went, since it was getting late and he was starting to get worried.

Phoebe shook her head instinctively, then remembered that Adrian couldn't see her. She texted him back and said "I'm not helping you find Erica. Like I said, I don't care if she wants to play hooky, but you're not dragging me into this."

Instead of texting Phoebe again, Adrian chose to call her. To which Phoebe responded to with an irritable "What?"

"Phoebe, come on," said Adrian. "You can't convince me that you aren't the least bit worried about Erica."

"No, I'm not," said Phoebe firmly. "If she wants to skip school, that is her problem, for the last time. Now stop bothering me about it." Phoebe hung up the phone before Adrian could say anything else, but deep inside, she knew that she was lying to both herself and Adrian.

She really was concerned for Erica, but she also didn't want to get dragged into this kind of mess, no matter what the reason for Erica skipping school was. Frankly, she was more than content to let Erica handle it herself and leave everybody else out of it, especially her.

"Am I being a terrible friend by not helping find Erica?" Phoebe wondered to herself. "Is it better to just stay out of this altogether or should I help Adrian and Scott?"

It was a question she couldn't answer definitively, but for the time being, she decided it was better to just stay out of it. After all, getting involved in something like this could mess up her school record, and she wanted to keep a perfect school record all throughout high school.

"Besides," she said to herself, trying to convince herself that what she was doing was right, "I'm younger than Erica. It's not my responsibility to figure out where she goes and what she does."

Phoebe walked back to her room and picked her book up off her bed. "I'm sure she'll be fine," she said to herself, trying to go back to reading her book.

Chapter III

Scott was at Adrian's house in a few minutes. Adrian asked Scott, "Okay, so what exactly do you want to do? It's not like we can track Erica. And where's Phoebe?"

"I couldn't get Phoebe to come," said Scott. "She won't help, since she thinks Erica purposefully skipped school, and she doesn't want to get involved."

"Well, I'm not sure that I blame her," said Adrian. "I mean, why else would Erica be gone all day?"

"I don't know," said Scott. "But I refuse to believe that Erica just went and skipped school like that. She's never done something like that before, and unless there was an emergency of some kind, I don't think that she'd have any real reason to."

"Okay, that's true, but still... What do you hope to find out by sitting here and talking?" Adrian asked.

"I want to retrace her steps," said Scott. "I saw her last night, and her mom said that she saw her this morning," so she definitely went home last night.

"And her mom said that she left for school this morning, but nobody saw her at school," Adrian continued.

"Which means that somewhere along the route to school, something happened, and she never made it to school," Scott finished.

"It's like a 5-to-10-minute walk to school from Erica's house," said Adrian. "What could have happened to her?"

"I don't know," said Scott. "Maybe you're right. Maybe she did just decide to skip school for whatever reason. Maybe this is all just a big waste of time."

"You don't believe any of that, do you?" asked Adrian.

Scott sighed. "No, I don't. I can't bring myself to believe that Erica would purposefully skip school and not come home for hours without picking up her cell phone or telling anyone where she was going."

"So, what's left?" asked Adrian. "You don't think she was..." Adrian trailed off.

"Was what?" asked Scott.

"I don't know, it was just a thought," said Adrian.

"Well, come on. Tell me what you were thinking," Scott demanded.

"It seems ridiculous, but do you think it's possible that Erica was kidnapped?" Adrian suggested. "I know it seems farfetched, but it's certainly seems possible, given the situation."

Scott raised his eyebrows. "Kidnapped?" he asked. "Why would someone kidnap Erica. Her parents aren't rich, and it's not like we live in a particularly dangerous neighborhood."

Adrian shrugged. "I know. It sounds ridiculous, but we should talk to Officer McKinley just in case."

"I'm sure that Erica's parents have already reported her missing by now," Scott said. "There's not really anything that we can tell him that he probably doesn't already know."

"Look, it's going to get dark in a few minutes," said Adrian. "My parents are going to get home soon and you should probably head home before it gets too dark to bike."

Scott stood up. "Yeah, you're right. I just wish that there was something that we could do."

"So do I," said Adrian. "But I'm sure nothing's happened to Erica. Remember, like you said, we live don't live in a dangerous town, and Erica knows how to defend herself. She's probably the best fighter I've ever met."

Scott chuckled. "Yeah, you don't want to be on the receiving end of her fist." He grabbed his backpack and headed towards the door. "I'll see you tomorrow."

Adrian waved goodbye and Scott grabbed his bike and headed home. It only took him about 10 minutes, but by the time he got home, it was already dark out. It was also starting to get cold, which only made Scott more concerned. He tried calling Erica again, but once again got no response.

His parents would probably be home in about half an hour, since the store was closed and they were probably just cleaning up. Scott opened the fridge and pulled out a loaf of bread. He cut himself off a couple of slices and stuck them in the toaster.

There wasn't much for him to do. He had finished his homework and he really didn't feel like reading. So instead of standing around, doing nothing, waiting for his parents to come home, he decided to practice his guitar.

He got his guitar from his room, took a seat on the couch, and started playing some chords and practicing a song he was learning.

Meanwhile, Phoebe was trying to finish her book, but she simply couldn't concentrate on the book. She had been on the same chapter for the past hour and she still didn't know what was happening.

She stuck the bookmark back in the book again and slipped it back on to the bookshelf. "What's the matter with me?" she asked herself. "Erica's not your problem. Stop thinking about her."

It wasn't working, though. Her thoughts kept turning back to Erica's whereabouts, no matter how much she tried to push them away. In an effort to clear her mind, Phoebe opened her window and stared at the night sky. Whenever she was distracted or stuck on a problem, Phoebe often found the counting the stars in the sky helped her focus.

Tonight was different. She couldn't even manage to keep track of what number she was on, much less which stars she had counted. Annoyed with herself, Phoebe checked her watch and realized that it was already 8 o'clock.

Her parents had come home about an hour ago, but they were in the study working out the finances for their company. The fact that it was so late made Phoebe realize that Erica had been gone for the entire day now, which, even Phoebe had to admit, was completely unlike Erica.

Phoebe was about to shut her window and call Scott to ask him if he had heard from Erica at all, when the motion sensor lights mounted on her driveway turned on. Curious, Phoebe peered out the window to see who had triggered the lights.

Even with the light, though, it was too dark to see much. Phoebe thought that she could see a figure walking down the street away from her house, but she couldn't see his or her face. It also didn't help that she was on the second floor, which made it even harder for her to see anything on the ground below.

"Erica?" Phoebe called out from the window. The figure stopped walking, and Phoebe thought that she saw the person look up at her. She called Erica's name again.

There was no answer, and the person turned away from the window and continued to walk away. Confused, Phoebe walked away from the window and headed downstairs to see who was out there. She left the house and walked over to the driveway, where she saw the person walking away.

"Hey, stop!" Phoebe yelled to the person. "Who are you?" When the person didn't respond, Phoebe started to run after the person, but as soon as the person noticed Phoebe, they took off running as well.

Phoebe groaned and tore after the person, but she wasn't much of a runner, and the person was much faster than her. Plus, they had a decent head start, which didn't really help things.

The person was running down a street with streetlamps now, though, and Phoebe could see the person better. It was a girl, but Phoebe could tell simply by the way that she was running that it was Erica.

"Erica, stop!" Phoebe yelled, breathing heavily. "I know it's you! What's going on."

Surprisingly, the person stopped running and turned around suddenly, almost causing Phoebe to run straight into them. Now that she was close enough to the person, and along with the light from the streetlamp, Phoebe could see the person clearly.

It was indeed Erica, but she was a mess. Her clothes were torn, she had bruises all over as well as cuts and scrapes everywhere.

"Erica, what happened to you?" Phoebe asked. "Where have you been? What's going on?"

"Nothing happened," said Erica. "I just went to some sports thing."

"But you're a mess," Phoebe protested. "You look like you just went to a wrestling match."

"I'm fine, okay," said Erica. "I just fell off my bike."

"You didn't take your bike with you, though," said Phoebe. "You left it in your garage."

"Well, it wasn't my bike, it was someone else's, alright," said Erica.

"Why were you running away from me?" asked Phoebe. "You're not telling me something!"

"I just didn't want to talk to you, alright?" Erica snapped. "Now leave me alone."

Taken aback, Phoebe said "What's up with you. You're completely different. You've never acted like this before."

"Nothing up with me," said Erica. "I'm fine." Erica walked away, leaving Phoebe alone, wondering what had just happened. Confused, and unsure what to do, Phoebe walked back home and called Scott and Adrian and told them how she had just seen Erica.

"Is she okay?" asked Adrian. "Where did she go?"

"She's okay, but she's all cut and bruised," said Phoebe. "She said that she went to a "sports thing" and fell off a bike, but even I could tell that she was lying."

"That doesn't make sense," said Scott. "Why would she lie about where she was? And why would she skip school for something like that?"

"I have no idea," said Phoebe. "And she's not herself. She's really irritable and just altogether, different."

"What do you mean by "different"? asked Scott.

"I don't know how to explain it," said Phoebe. "You'll probably see what I mean tomorrow at school, assuming she's there."

"I don't understand this," said Adrian. "First, she disappears for an entire day, and then she comes back all cut up and you say she's different?"

"I don't understand it either, but she's clearly hiding something," said Phoebe. "However, I don't have a clue what it is."

"This is all really strange," said Scott. "I've gotta go, though. I'll see you tomorrow."

"Yeah, me too," said Adrian. "I'll see if I can talk to Erica tomorrow."

They all said goodbye and hung up the phone, each of them wondering what was going on.

Chapter IV

It was the next day and the three of them were standing in the school parking lot a few minutes before school was about to start.

"Have you seen Erica yet?" Scott asked.

Adrian nodded. "I saw her go inside a few minutes ago. Phoebe's right. She looks terrible. Something happened last night that she's not telling us about."

"I told you," said Phoebe. "There's no way she could be that badly hurt by just falling off a bike."

"Yeah, I-." Scott was interrupted by the bell ringing, indicating that it was time to go to class. "Okay, we gotta go," he said, dashing towards the entrance with Phoebe and Adrian close behind him.

Scott, Adrian, and Phoebe watched Erica throughout all their classes, but nothing seemed strange. She took her classes normally, and even raised her hand to answer questions. At the end of P.E., Scott, Adrian, and Phoebe all went to the cafeteria to eat lunch, along with everybody else.

Scott intended to find Erica during lunch and ask her some questions, but when they all sat down at the table, he couldn't find Erica anywhere.

"Phoebe, did you see Erica come in at all?" he asked.

Phoebe shook her head. "I saw her in P.E. but after that, I lost her in the crowd of people going to the cafeteria."

"Where would she go?" asked Adrian. "We just saw her."

"I don't know..." Scott said, scanning the room. "Wait, there!" Scott pointed in the direction of the exit. "Come on, let's go." Scott took off running, leaving Adrian and Phoebe very confused.

Scott dashed towards to exit, almost barreling down a student holding a lunch tray.

"Hey, watch where you're going, idiot," the kid yelled.

"Sorry, about that," Scott called back, not taking his eyes off Erica. He was almost close enough to her, but suddenly Erica noticed him and took off running. Scott was prepared for this, though and slid a lunch tray towards Erica, causing her to slip on it and fall. Scott ran over to her and caught her before her head slammed into the ground.

"Okay, what's going on, Erica?" he demanded. "You were completely gone yesterday, and now you're acting completely out of character. What gives?"

"Nothing, okay," said Erica, getting to her feet, "There's nothing going on."

"Oh, so you just felt like going for a stroll during lunch period?" asked Adrian, who, followed by Phoebe, can come up behind Scott.

"Look, there's nothing going on!" Erica said, "What do you want from me?"

"Erica, we're worried about you," broke in Phoebe. "You've never acted like this before. "There's obviously something happening with you that you're not telling us. All these cuts, bruises. You disappearing and running away from all of us. You need to tell someone what's happening, if not us."

"I told you already. I got these cuts from falling off a bike and I went to a sports event yesterday," Erica said.

"Don't be ridiculous," said Scott. "Nobody believes that story at all. Just tell us where you really went and what really happened."

"Nothing!" Erica burst out. Suddenly, she shoved Scott away and ran down the hallway towards the exit.

Adrian looked at Scott and Phoebe. "So, do we go after her, or what?" he asked.

Scott shook his head. "Forget it. Even if we did chase after her, she's too fast. Let's just wait until school ends to talk to her again. We have to get back before the lunch bell rings, anyway."

The three of them walked back to the lunch table and finished their lunches, while all thinking about what could be happening with Erica. After the lunch bell rang, they all went to their respective classes, and Scott was surprise to see Erica in his Biology class, which was right after lunch period.

"Where did she go?" he wondered to himself. "And how did she get back so soon?"

The questions would have to be put on hold, though, since he was supposed to be learning about the digestive system of certain types of fish, and naturally, the biology teacher demanded his full attention.

As school as the final bell rang, Scott tried to track down Erica in the halls, but she wasn't anywhere. Instead, he ran into Adrian and Phoebe, also looking for Erica.

"Did you find her?" Scott asked.

Adrian and Phoebe both shook their heads. "Nope, it looks like she made it out before us."

"Okay, what is going on?!" exclaimed Scott. "Something happened to Erica yesterday. I don't know what it was, but I'm going to figure it out."

"We're with you," said Adrian. "But if Erica won't talk to us, then there's nothing we can do."

"We've been friends for over 10 years," said Scott. "If there's something wrong, why wouldn't she tell us?"

"I don't know that, either," said Phoebe, "But if Erica won't talk to us, the only thing that we can do is figure out where she keeps going by ourselves."

"So, what do you propose we do?" asked Scott. "She keeps disappearing the minute we stop watching her."

"She looks nervous all the time, too," said Adrian. "I don't know if you guys noticed that, but she looks like she's worried about something every time I see her."

"Okay, so all we have to do is watch her during school and follow her to see where she goes when she leaves," said Phoebe. "We just can't let her out of our sight after the bell rings."

"That works, but she takes a different class then the rest of us," Scott said. "Erica's last class before the bell rings is French, and none of us take that."

"True, but Spanish class always ends about 3 minutes before the bell rings," said Adrian. "Since that's my last class, I should be able to leave the classroom and still have enough time to get to the classroom where French class is held before Erica leaves."

"Okay, and we'll meet you outside in the parking lot," said Phoebe. "Just don't let Erica see you."

"Alright, perfect," said Scott. "I'll see you guys tomorrow. Normally I'd want to discuss this more in detail with you guys at one of our houses, but my parents said they need my help at the store, and that means that I'll probably be there all day once I'm done with my homework."

"That's fine, since I have to help Katie with her math, anyway," Adrian said, mentally groaning just thinking about it.

"And I might as well work on my latest project, since I don't have anything better to do," said Phoebe.

The three friends said goodbye, and then all headed home, going in separate ways at the next intersection.

Chapter V

Once Adrian arrived home, there wasn't a whole lot for him to do, besides homework and chores. But the whole thing with Erica was really getting to him, so much so that it prevented him from concentrating on his homework.

Adrian prided himself on being logical (although not as much as Phoebe), but this situation really didn't make any logical sense at all.

Instead of doing his homework, since he couldn't concentrate anyway, he decided to go over what he knew about what had happened to Erica. He grabbed a piece of paper out from his desk drawer and started drawing up a graph.

"Okay, so let's see," he muttered to himself, "We know Scott saw her two days ago and she was perfectly normal. Then her mother saw her again yesterday morning and she was still normal. Then she went to school, but somewhere on the way, she changed courses."

Adrian sketched out a path that showed the route that Erica would have taken. "Okay, so we also know that she came back last night, but Phoebe says that she was different," he said to himself. "And now she's completely different and keeps disappearing."

Adrian studied the paper for a while, but simply couldn't make sense of the facts. The only way this was ever going to make sense, was if they learned where Erica had been 2 days ago.

"Whatcha doing?" Katie asked, creeping up behind Adrian. "Can I join?"

Startled, Adrian jumped, causing Katie to laugh. "Ha! Scared ya!"

Adrian sighed and stuck the paper back into his desk drawer and asked "What do you want, Katie?"

"Mom says you need to help me with my homework now," Katie answered, sticking a piece of paper in Adrian face.

Adrian pushed the paper away and said "I haven't even finished my own homework yet," he said to Katie, "Can you give me about an hour?"

Katie shook her head. "Nope, I have a tea party to go to in an hour. You gotta help me now."

Adrian grunted. "Alright, fine. Take a seat," he said, putting the paper on the desk.

The rest of Adrian's day was awfully dull. He spent about an hour "tutoring" Katie, and the rest of the time doing his homework. When nighttime came, he went straight to bed the minute it got dark outside.

Of course, he couldn't fall asleep anyway, so instead of actually sleeping, he lay awake staring at his ceiling thinking about Erica and everything else that had happened, until his brain got too full of thoughts and he conked out.

PHOEBE GOT HOME IN a few minutes, since her house was closest to the school. Neither of her parents were home yet, which meant that she had plenty of time to do her homework and work on her science project.

Phoebe went upstairs to her bedroom and tossed her backpack onto her bed. She dug out her homework folder and put it on her desk, trying to keep the events of the day out of her mind so she could focus on her homework.

She was only human, though, and it was pretty hard to ignore the fact that one of your best friends had turned into a completely different person in the span of only one day. So, despite all her attempts, she simply couldn't stop thinking about it.

She had run through all the possible scenarios that she could think of in her head, but nothing seemed to logically add up. Clearly, Erica hadn't been kidnapped, since she had returned home, and it didn't seem logical that she was telling the truth and had truly just gone to a sports event.

"So, what happened?" Phoebe asked herself. "This doesn't make any sense." Phoebe wasn't used to things not making any sense and hated it when there was a problem that she couldn't solve.

Trying to take her thoughts away from Erica, Phoebe took her Rubik's cube off her shelf and started solving it. It was a habit that she had developed a few years ago, and she had gotten so good at solving Rubik's cubes that it only took her about 30 seconds to a minute to solve one.

Solving the Rubik's cube helped. Phoebe was able to clear her thoughts and concentrate on her homework. She finished her homework in less than an hour, like always, and decided that she might as well get started on her science project.

It was a basic project by Phoebe's standards, but since it was assigned to her, she didn't really have much of a choice. She had tried to ask the teacher if she could do a harder project, but the teacher had told her that he was tired of giving her different projects and it was time for her to do the assigned project.

She was in the middle of writing a blurb for her poster, when the doorbell rang. Confused about who would be at the door at this time, Phoebe reluctantly left her project and went downstairs.

She opened the door and was surprised to a random man standing there. "Can I help you with something?" Phoebe asked.

The man looked at a piece of paper he was holding and said "Is there an Erica Feldman here?"

Phoebe gulped. Stunned and unsure of what to do, she said "No, nobody by that name lives here."

The man scratched his head. "Okay, do you know where I can find her?"

Phoebe had no idea what was going on, but she certainly wasn't about to give this random man Erica's address. "Sorry, I've never heard that name before."

The man shrugged. "Alright, well, thanks anyway, I guess."

Phoebe gave a fake smile and said "Yep, no problem," just wishing the guy would go away so she could close the door. She didn't know what it was, but something seemed off about this guy.

Thankfully, the man gave a small wave and walked away. Immediately, Phoebe shut the door and locked it, making sure to engage the deadbolt.

"Okay, Erica has got herself mixed up in something awful," she thought to herself. "We need to figure out what's going on, ASAP."

Breathing heavily, Phoebe tried to calm herself down by telling herself that everything was fine, but she knew that it wasn't.

"Okay, what do I do, what do I do?" Phoebe asked herself again and again. She considered texting Adrian and Scott, but she knew they would want to come over, and she didn't want to bring them into this.

Phoebe decided that the best thing for her to do right now would be to take a warm shower. She found them relaxing, and something relaxing was just what she needed right now. It worked. After taking a shower, Phoebe felt much calmer and was able to finish her science project without any other incidents.

She almost had a heart attack when her parents came home, since she thought they were intruders, but after eating some dinner, she decided to go to bed early so she would be prepared for tomorrow.

AS FOR SCOTT, HIS DAY was pretty much planned out for him. Once he got home, he put on the uniform that his parents gave him for when he helped out at the store and tossed his homework on his desk, intending to get it done later.

He left his room and hopped on his bike. It was only a 15-minute bike ride to the store, but the wind was against him, so it took him an extra few minutes. When he got to the store, he could see why his parents needed help. There were so many people in the store, that there was a long line forming at the checkout.

Scott pushed his way towards the checkout where he found his mom scanning items as fast as she could.

"Mom, what do you need my help with?" Scott asked.

"Oh, Scott. Thanks goodness," Scott's mom responded without looking up from her scanning. "This place is a madhouse. Take over the third register."

"Sure," said Scott, walking behind the counter and opening the register. Right away, a line started forming in front of his register and Scott got to scanning items immediately.

"Where's Dad?" Scott asked his mom while scanning 16 sticks of butter.

Scott's mom gestured to the crowd. "He's out there restocking shelves. I don't know why everybody is buying so much stuff all of a sudden."

Scott shrugged. "I don't know, but it's good for business." He made a face as someone placed 5 pounds of blue cheese on the counter.

Scott had been working for about an hour and the crowds were finally starting to subside. His arm was also starting to hurt from constantly scanning items.

"Hey Mom, can I switch places with Dad?" Scott asked. "He can scan items and I'll restock."

Scott's mom nodded. "Sure, go find him and ask him to switch."

"Thanks!" Scott closed off the register and went to go find dad. He found him in the freezer section, restocking vanilla ice cream.

"Hey Dad, can you take my spot at the register?" Scott asked. "I'll take over restocking."

Scott's dad put down the ice cream he was holding and said "Of course." He chuckled. "My hands are freezing anyway."

He handed gestured to the cart next to him and said "Just put these in the right places. When you run out, you can go to the back. One of the workers will give you some more stuff."

Scott's dad walked over to the registers, leaving Scott to stock the ice cream by himself. He started putting things on the shelves. He emptied out the cart in a few minutes and he was about to go to the back when he noticed Erica in the produce aisle.

Scott pushed his cart off to the side and walked over to Erica to try and talk to her.

"Erica!" Scott said "What are you doing here?" Erica jumped and turned around, startled.

"Scott, please. Leave me alone," Erica said. "I'm just here to pick up some vegetables for my mom."

"No, Erica. What's going on with you?" he asked. "I know we've all asked you this before, but you've never given us an answer."

"I have," said Erica. "Nothing."

"Come on, tell me something," Scott said. "Look, I need to keep stocking shelves or my parents will get mad, but if you're in trouble, you really need to tell someone."

Erica opened her mouth like she was about to say something, then shook her head. "I'm not in trouble. I've just been feeling aggravated lately."

"Aggravated? About what?" Scott asked.

"I don't know. Stuff," Erica replied. "Just go away and let me get these carrots for the soup."

Scott shrugged. "Alright then. If you don't want to tell me, that fine. But you really *should tell someone*."

Erica nodded and started picking through the carrots, pulling out the biggest ones there was.

Scott started to walk away and then stopped and said "I forgot to ask you." Erica looked up from the carrots. "If this is about me again- "

Scott held up his hand. "Nothing to do with that," he said. "I just wanted to ask you if you heard about Old Man McGinnis. Did you know that he got robbed?"

Erica suddenly froze and dropped the carrot she was holding. She put her hand to her mouth and looked like she was about to throw up. Then she took off running towards the utility sink in the back of the store.

Unsure of what just happened, Scott abandoned his shelving job and chased after Erica. "Erica! What happened?" he called after her, gaining a couple of looks from people still shopping.

Scott ran into the back room where he found Erica standing over the sink, washing her face. Scott slowly walked over to her and asked "Erica, are you okay?"

Erica raised her head from the sink and shook her head. "No, I'm not. There's something you need to know." She looked around the room and asked "Are the walls of these place concrete or metal?"

Confused, Scott nodded. "It was originally a factory. There's no windows and the walls are made out of concrete."

"Perfect." Erica walked over to a corner of the room and gestured for Scott to follow her. Scott did so, though he wasn't sure what was going on. Erica took a seat in the corner and said "You guys were right. There is something going on."

Erica rolled up her pant leg to reveal a device that was strapped to her ankle. Still confused, Scott asked "What is shat?"

"It's a long story," she said.

"Well, you should start now," said Scott. "No matter how long it takes."

Erica bit her lip and nodded. "Where do I start?" she asked.

"Well, where you were 2 days ago would be great," said Scott.

Erica nodded. "Okay, let me tell you. Just don't interrupt me."

"Okay, I can do that," said Scott.

Erica started, "I was walking to school on Wednesday, two days ago, when I was approached by two men, both wearing masks. Whenever you see people wearing masks, you know things are bad, so I tried to run, but one of them grabbed my leg and I fell.

I think one of them hit me on the head with something, because that's the last thing I remember before I woke up in some old warehouse tied to a chair. The two men, still wearing masks walked over to me and told me that they needed me for something

I asked what it was, and they said they needed my help in a robbery. Naturally, I refused, but of them brought out a gun and told me if I didn't help, I would be shot right there and then. I begged them to let me go, but they told me that I was the perfect person for the job.

Since I didn't really want to get shot, I agreed to help them. I didn't want to, but I didn't have much of another option. Then they strapped this modified ankle monitor on me. It has a tracker and a mic on it, so they always know where I am, and they can always hear me.

Then they took me to a house. It was McGinnis' house. They told me how the robbery was supposed to go, and swore that if I didn't follow their instructions, they wouldn't hesitate to kill me. They cut open one of the windows with some special knife and told me climb through.

I cut my arm and leg climbing through the window, but eventually I was able to locate the things that they wanted to steal. I put it all in a bag and climbed back out the window, getting more cuts. I handed them the bag and asked if they could let me go, now that I did what I was supposed to.

They laughed and said that my job wasn't over yet. They told me that they still needed me to deliver the stolen goods to other people. In fact, they said that would be my job from now on and if I told anyone, the mic would let them know and they'd find me and kill me. So, that's where I've been going all the time and why I can't tell anyone."

Erica took a deep breath after telling this story and Scott noticed that there were tears running down her cheek.

Scott was shocked. He knew something was going on with Erica, but he had never imagined something like this. "I don't know what to say," he said. "That-that's horrible. You need to tell Officer McKinley."

"No, no, I can't," said Erica. "That's the point. If I tell anyone, they'll *kill* me."

"But you're telling me now, aren't you?" asked Scott.

"We're in a concrete building," said Erica. "The computer or whatever they use can't connect to the ankle monitor when the signal is blocked. So, all they hear now is static. Which means they are probably getting suspicious."

"Okay, so how about I tell Officer McKinley?" Scott asked. "They can't hear me."

"No, but if they find out I told you and you told McKinley, they'll find me and..." Erica trailed off before she could finish her sentence.

"But you can't keep doing what they say," said Scott. "Can we get the lock off?"

Erica shook her head. "It's a combination lock. And it's 4 digits, so there's over a thousand different combinations. And I don't want to do what they say, but I don't have much of a choice."

Erica stood up. "I need to get out of here or they'll start getting suspicious." She started walking towards the exit and Scott followed her.

"Look, you have to tell someone," said Scott. "If you tell Officer McKinley, I'm sure he'll be able to keep you safe.

Erica stopped walking. "What do you mean by 'keep me safe'" she asked.

"Well, maybe they can have an officer stand watch near your house or you can stay at the police station," said Scott. "Besides, I'm sure that they have something that can remove the ankle monitor."

"Maybe," said Erica. "But what if they can't keep me safe and the thieves come after me again. Then what?"

Scott was at a loss for words. "I don't know," he said. "But just don't think about that. I'm sure that you're going to be fine."

Erica shook her head. "I'm not risking that. I think it's better if you guys just stay away from me and keep yourselves away from danger."

"No!" Scott said adamantly. "That's not right. It's not what friends do, and I'm sure Phoebe and Adrian would agree with me."

"Don't bring them into this too," said Erica. "Look, it's bad enough that you know, but as long as you don't tell anyone else, you'll be fine."

"What about you?" asked Scott. "I'm not just going to give up."

"There's nothing you, Adrian, Phoebe, or Officer McKinley can do," said Erica. She wiped her face with her hand and said "Look, I appreciate you trying to help, but the more you get involved, the more danger you put yourself and me in."

"Erica..."

Erica held up her hand. "This is just how it is now," she said. "I guess I'm just a criminal now."

"At the very least, you can tell me whose house they intend to target next. That way we can have the police wait outside the house to catch them," Scott suggested.

"I don't know what the next house they intend to rob is," said Erica. "They don't tell me where I'm going until we're there."

Erica walked over towards the door and said "Scott, we've been friends for years, but I can't be with you or anybody else anymore without putting you in danger. I'm sorry, but you're going to help to forget me as a friend."

"No, I won't accept that," said Scott. "You can't just give everything up because of two crazy thieves."

Erica shook her head. "Until somebody threatens to kill you unless you help them, you'll never understand." She opened the heavy steel door and walked back into the store, leaving Scott helplessly trying to grasp what had just happened.

"Scott!" a voice called out from the store, making Scott jump out of his trance. Scott's dad poked his head through the doors. "What happened to restocking the shelves?" he asked. "You can chit-chat later. Duty calls!"

Scott nodded. "Yeah, sorry Dad. I'll get on it." Scott left the warehouse and walked back over to the cart, intending to refill it. His mind was completely focused on what Erica had just told him, though.

He knew that Erica was right and if he told anybody, he'd be putting not only his and their life in danger, but also Erica's.

"But I can't just do nothing," Scott thought to himself. "Somebody needs to know." He tossed a couple of packages of bacon in the freezer and tried to make a decision. Scott argued with himself back and forth for a few minutes, but he simply couldn't come to a decision.

On one hand, he couldn't accept the fact that Erica was just going to be a criminal's assistant forever, but on the other hand, he didn't want to put her in danger by telling Officer McKinley or anyone for that matter.

Finally, Scott decided on a solution. "Erica's smart," he told himself. "She'll find a way out of this, I'm sure." He decided that he wouldn't tell anyone, but if the situation kept getting worse and Erica started disappearing for longer times, he would have to tell someone.

Convincing himself that this was the best solution was only the first part, though. He still had to keep himself from telling anyone until he deemed it necessary. That would be a challenge, especially when Adrian and Phoebe started asking Erica where she was.

To distract himself, Scott buried himself into his work until the store closed. Then he headed home and did his homework. It wouldn't be entirely truthful to say that he didn't think about Erica at all, but he was able to put it out of his mind until tomorrow morning at school.

Chapter VI

Scott met up with Phoebe in the school parking lot. He was about to greet Phoebe when he caught a glimpse of Erica walking into the school, and all the thoughts from yesterday came back. He didn't realize how hard he was thinking until Phoebe snapped her fingers in his face.

"Uh, hello, Earth to Scott," she said. Scott shook his head and said "Sorry, what were you saying?"

Phoebe said "I was just asking if you saw Erica at all yesterday. I didn't and neither did Adrian."

Scott instantly shook his head. "Nope, didn't see her. Why do you ask?"

Phoebe was a little confused by Scott's response, but she brushed it off as him being distracted. She said, "I was just curious. Hopefully, she's at school today. Is something up with you?"

"I think I just saw her walk in," said Scott. "What do you mean by "something up with me?""

"You seem, I don't know, sort of out of it," Phoebe responded. "Doesn't matter. Adrian's already inside. Let's go find Erica."

"Yeah, about that," said Scott. "How about you two just follow Erica? I've gotta focus on my schoolwork and some of my grades up."

Phoebe stared at him. "The school year just started. You don't even know what your grades are yet."

Scott shrugged. "Well, you know what I mean, right? Grades, schoolwork, homework, all that stuff..."

Phoebe shook her head. "No, I have no idea what you mean. And what in the world is up with you?" she asked. "You're acting almost as weird as Erica. Did she put you in some sort of trance?"

Scott laughed nervously. "What-what do you mean? I'm perfectly normal."

"You suck at lying, Scott," Phoebe said with a look on her face that meant "Are you being serious right now?" "What in the world is going on? We really don't need two friends acting strange."

"No clue what you mean," said Scott. "No-." Scott was interrupted by the school bell ringing. "Well, looks like it's time to go to class," he said. "See you later, Phoebe." Scott dashed off into the school leaving Phoebe behind.

"What is happening?" Phoebe asked herself. "First Erica, now Scott. Something strange is going on here." Phoebe didn't have much time to ponder about the strangeness of Erica and Scott, though, since the second bell rang, indicating that if the students didn't get their butt inside now, they'd get a tardiness report.

"Shoot!" Phoebe said out loud. She grabbed her backpack off the bench and hurried into school. She intended to meet up with Adrian and Scott during lunch so they could follow Erica and see if she left again during lunch period.

After P.E, which all of them were in, Phoebe found Adrian and said "See if you can find Erica. I'm going to go find Scott."

"Okay," Adrian said. "I think I saw Erica going to the lunch line. Also, what's up with Scott? He acted all weird when I mentioned Erica."

Phoebe shrugged. "No idea. He was like that with me too. Something's going on."

"Yeah, I can tell." Adrian sounded irritated. "I'm really missing summer vacation now."

Phoebe laughed. "I'm starting to agree with you. As much as I like school, I just want everything to go back to normal."

Adrian nodded. "Yeah. Anyway, I'm going to go find Erica. Text me when you find Scott and I'll let you know where I am." Adrian left the gym and went off to find Erica while Phoebe hunted for Scott.

Adrian spotted Erica standing in the lunch line holding an empty tray. He stayed a few feet away from her so she couldn't see him and watched what she was doing. Nothing out of the ordinary happened, though. Erica got her food from the lunch lady and took a seat at one of the tables.

Adrian continued to watch her, waiting for her to get up and leave the hall or for something to happen, but nothing happened. Adrian texted Phoebe and Scott, letting them know what table he was at, and that nothing was happening.

As he was watching, he noticed Erica take out her phone, but Adrian couldn't see what she was doing. Suddenly, she got up and abandoned her food, and walked towards the exit. Making sure to stay a few feet behind, Adrian followed Erica, but he didn't get very far before he ran into Scott.

"Scott, Erica is leaving again," Adrian said to Scott. "We need to figure out where she's going."

To Adrian's surprise, Scott shook his head and said "No, let her go."

"What are you talking about?" Adrian demanded. "We agreed that we would follow Erica and find out where she keeps going."

"Maybe it's better if we don't know," said Scott. "I've been thinking about it, and I've decided that it's Erica's business where she goes and not ours."

"True, but she's our friend," Adrian protested. "Shouldn't we know if she's in trouble or something?"

"She's our friend, so we should respect her privacy," said Scott. "If she doesn't want us to know where she's going, then we shouldn't keep snooping."

"But she's leaving school," Adrian said. "Shouldn't we at least tell Principal Peterson?"

"Well, we don't know for sure that she's leaving school," said Scott. "We never saw her."

"What? Yes, we did," said Adrian. "She left through the hallway exit yesterday. What has got into you?" he demanded.

"Nothing," Scott said "I just think that we should let Erica be."

Phoebe walked up behind Scott and Adrian and asked "Where's Erica? I thought you said she was sitting at that table." She gestured to the table that Adrian had told them about.

"She left," said Adrian. "And Scott won't let me follow him." He glared at Scott.

"Okay, Scott, this is ridiculous," Phoebe said. "Between you and Erica something is going on. I wasn't going to tell you this, but yesterday night, some random man came to my house and asked for Erica. When I told him she wasn't there, he asked for her address. I told him I didn't know anybody Erica. So, what is going on? And don't tell me nothing, because that's a complete lie."

Finally, Scott decided there was no better option except to tell them what had happened to Erica, since it wasn't like they were going to take no for an answer, anyway.

"Alright, I'll admit. There is something going on," he said. "If you meet me at my house after school, I'll tell you about it."

Adrian and Phoebe looked confused. "Why can't you just tell us here?" Adrian asked.

Scott shook his head. "There are too many people here. Just come to my house later and I'll explain."

Phoebe shrugged. "Alright," she said. "But you'd better have a good explanation."

Phoebe walked away, back to the lunch table, leaving Scott alone with Adrian.

"Well, we should get back to lunch and get something to eat before the bell rings," Scott suggested, trying to change the topic.

Adrian nodded. "Yeah, okay." He followed Phoebe back to the lunch table. "I'll see you after school, though."

After Adrian had left, Scott took a deep breath and thought to himself "This is a bad idea. What happens if Erica finds out I told them. Or worse, what happens if the thieves forcing her to commit crimes find out she told me."

Right now, though, Scott was more concerned for Erica. He didn't know where she had gone, and he could only hope that what she was doing wasn't dangerous. And even if it was, there wasn't anything he could do about it.

Scott went back to his table to finish his lunch, but he was only able to get in a few bites before the lunch bell rang. When he went back to class, he didn't see Erica there, which was concerning, but he told himself that she was fine.

Scott didn't see Erica at all for the rest of school, but as soon as the bell rang, he was approached by Adrian and Phoebe.

"So, where's Erica?" Phoebe asked. "She hasn't been in any classes since lunch."

"I don't know," said Scott. "But if you guys follow me home, I'll promise I'll explain what's going on."

Adrian bunched his eyebrows. "I don't know..."

"Just do it," Scott said. "Seriously. Either you come with me now, or I'm not telling you."

"Alright, just let's just go get our bikes first," Adrian said. "Phoebe, you'll have to walk."

Phoebe rarely biked to school, since she lived about 3 minutes away from school. It was almost a 20-minute walk to Scott's house from school, though.

Phoebe shook her head. "I'll grab my bike from my house when I pass it. I'll see you two in a bit."

"Okay, sounds good," Scott and Adrian grabbed their bikes from the bike racks and pedaled away while Phoebe walked to her house.

As expected, Adrian and Scott arrived at Scott's house first and waited a few minutes outside until Phoebe arrived on her bike.

"Alright, we're here," Phoebe said, getting off her bike. "Now you owe us an explanation."

"Let's go inside," Scott said, gesturing to the front door. Phoebe parked her bike next to a tree and followed Adrian and Scott towards Scott's house. Scott dug his key out of his backpack and unlocked the door. When they walked in, Scott immediately noticed that there were things missing. Not minor things, either. Their family's TV was missing from the shelf where it always sat and so was his dad's laptop, which he distinctly remembered seeing sitting on the kitchen table before he left for school.

"Uhh, Scott. Didn't you used to have a TV here?" Adrian asked, pointing at the empty shelf.

Scott's head was spinning. "Yes! Yes, I did," he said. "Someone must have broken in while I was at school," he said. "My Dad's laptop is missing."

"You sure your parents didn't just move some stuff around?" Adrian asked.

"Nope, pretty sure that Scott's right," Phoebe said, pulling a curtain away from the window to reveal a large, cleanly cut hole in the window.

"Wow, that is a smooth cut," said Adrian. "Someone knew what they were doing."

"We should call Officer McKinley," Phoebe said, pulling her cell phone out. "And you should let your parents know, Scott."

"No, wait," Scott said, holding his hand up. There was something about the cut on the window that rang a bell for him. Still holding his hand up, he thought for about a minute before he remembered.

Back at the store, when he was talking to Erica, she had mentioned that the thieves had cut open the window with some special knife. She had said "cut open" not break open.

"Would this be the kind of damage that a knife like that would cause?" Scott wondered to himself.

"Scott, hellooo," Adrian said. "Can we call McKinley now?"

Scott shook his head. He knew that if Erica was truly involved in the break-in, the thieves would be smart enough to hide themselves from the cameras and make Erica do everything. Which meant that if the police looked at the footage, they'd assume that Erica was the criminal, since she would be the only one on camera.

Phoebe gave Scott a look. "What do you mean 'no'?" she asked. "We have to tell the police about this."

"No, we don't," Scott insisted. "Look, let me explain, okay. Go find a place to sit and I'll tell you what I've been hiding."

Adrian shrugged. "You know what. If anything, I'm more curious for an explanation about you guy's weird behavior after this break in, so you might as well tell us." He plopped down on the couch.

"What? No. I-you need to report this immediately," Phoebe said "It's-"

"Phoebe, come on. Don't tell me that you don't want to know what's been going on with Scott and Erica," said Adrian.

"No, well, yes, I do, but this is more important," said Phoebe.

"Well, they're related," said Scott. "And if you stop talking for a second, I'll explain."

Now Phoebe looked surprised. "They're related? What do you mean?"

"Let me explain!" Scott said, exasperated. "Geez."

Phoebe sighed and sat down on the couch next to Adrian. "This better be worth it," she muttered.

Scott ignored her and started talking. "So, I met Erica at my parent's store yesterday and..."

Scott explained how he had talked to Erica and he repeated the story that Erica had told him. He repeated it word for word, making sure not to leave out any important details.

"So, I think that Erica might have had something to do with this robbery," Scott concluded. "That's why I don't think we can tell Officer McKinley yet."

Adrian held up his hand. "Wait, hang on. You're telling me that this is the reason Erica has been missing school and acting weird."

"And you knew about this?" Phoebe asked.

"Well, yeah, but only since yesterday," said Scott. "And I didn't know whether or not I should tell you."

"So, why'd you decide to tell us?" Adrian asked. "Aren't you putting Erica in danger now?"

"No, not if nobody finds out that I told you," Scott said. "And nobody finds out that Erica told me."

"Okay, but you didn't answer my first question," Adrian said. "Why'd you decide to tell us?"

Scott shrugged. "I don't actually know. I wasn't going to, but when Phoebe mentioned the random man asking her about Erica, I figured it was probably time I told you, since you were more than likely going to find out anyway."

"That, and you're really bad at keeping secrets," Phoebe said. "But, putting that aside, what are we supposed to do?"

"I haven't figured that out yet," said Scott. "But first things first, let's watch the security camera footage. See if it maybe captured Erica or one of the other thieves. I think it uploaded the footage onto our home computer."

"That's a good idea," Phoebe agreed. "But we don't even know for sure that Erica was actually involved in this robbery at all."

"You're right," said Scott. "But that hole cut out from the window matches what Erica told me about when they robbed McGinnis' house." Scott walked into the office to view the footage, but he was in for a surprise.

"And...they took the computer as well," said Scott. "Great. They didn't even bother with the keyboard and mouse; just the computer."

"So...now what?" Adrian asked. "The footage is gone and so is half your stuff."

Scott chuckled. "Oh, the footage isn't gone," he said. "Remember how the car thieves last summer used to hack our security cameras?"

"How could I forget," said Phoebe.

"Well, I convinced my Dad to let me take a simple precaution to ensure something like that wouldn't happen again," Scott said, walking outside.

Confused, Adrian asked "What are you talking about?"

Scott traced a wire that was connected to the security camera mounted closest to the living room window and followed it over to a small panel on the side of the house. He pried around the edges of it until the panel came off, revealing a small door with a number pad on it.

Scott entered a code and the light on the pad flashed green. Scott pulled open the door while Adrian and Phoebe watched curiously, unsure of what Scott was doing. Behind the door was a hard drive with a wire connected to it. It was mounted to the wall, inside a little compartment that was basically just a hole cut into the side of the house.

"What is that?" Adrian asked.

Before Scott could answer, Phoebe broke in and said "I believe it's a hard drive that is connected to the security camera."

Scott nodded. "Yep. Instead of having the camera only upload its footage to the computer's hard drive, I got this hard drive and wired the camera up to it."

"You did this?" Adrian asked. "The compartment and all?"

"Well, me and my dad did," Scott said. "Greg helped as well. It only took about 3 hours or so."

"That's impressive," Phoebe said. "You could use this compartment to store all kinds of things, such as a backup house key, or jewelry."

Scott pulled a screwdriver out of his backpack and unmounted the hard drive from the wall. "I'll connect this to my laptop and we can get the footage off it from there."

"Are you sure that the thieves didn't take that as well?" Adrian asked.

"Of course they didn't," Scott said, pulling it out of his backpack. "I never leave my laptop at home. It comes with me pretty much everywhere."

The three of them went back inside, and Scott sat his laptop down on the coffee table. He connected the drive up to his laptop and opened the video that contained the footage from today.

"How do you know what time the robbery was committed?" Adrian asked. "We don't have time to watch all the footage."

"No, but I can skip around," said Scott, dragging his finger along the seek bar. "There!" He stopped the seek bar and the footage showed someone walking up to their house, holding a small tool in their hand.

"That's Erica," said Phoebe. "I can tell by her outfit and size."

They continued the video and watched as Erica sliced open the window and climbed in. There were no cameras inside the house, but they could see Erica passing things to someone off camera. Finally, she climbed back out of the window and disappeared from the footage.

Scott closed the video and said, "This is not good. If the police see this footage, they'll arrest Erica, which will give the real thieves time to get away."

"So, don't show it to the police," said Adrian.

"I don't have a choice," Scott said. "Look, my parents are going to come home and find everything missing. They're going to know that there was a robbery and want to see the footage. Then they'll show the footage to the police and they'll come after Erica."

"So, delete the footage," Phoebe said.

Scott and Adrian were both surprised by Phoebe's suggestion. "You think we should delete the footage?" Scott asked. "You? The same girl who follows every rule in the book and hates being around rulebreakers?"

Phoebe nodded. "I know, it's not something I would normally suggest, but I don't think we have a choice. If you let the cops see the footage, then Erica gets arrested, and the real thieves go free."

Scott highlighted the video file. "If I delete this file, I'll be interfering with a police investigation. That's a crime, and I could be arrested if they ever find out."

"Well, how much do you want to help Erica," Adrian asked.

"My dad, Greg, and I are the only ones who know that this hard drive exists," Scott continued. "If the footage is missing, I'll be the first person who'll be suspected."

"No, you won't," said Adrian. "Your house was robbed, and you were at school all day. Just say that you came home and found it like this."

Scott shook his head. "I'm not going to do it." He shut the laptop lid and shoved it in his backpack.

"But-," said Adrian and Phoebe at the same time.

"I'm going to do this the right way," Scott said. "I'm just going to tell Officer McKinley what I just told you and show him the footage. He can explain everything to my parents."

"Okay, but what if the thieves find out that Erica told you?" Phoebe asked. "And they-"

"They won't," Scott said.

"You can't know that for sure," said Adrian. "There's always-"

"Stop, okay," said Scott. "Nothing is going to happen. They're just going to catch whoever is behind this and Erica will be fine. Now let's go to the police station before my parents get home."

"If you're sure about this," said Adrian, but he didn't sound convinced. Phoebe wasn't convinced either, but she followed Scott and Adrian out the door.

They each hopped on their bikes and headed for the police station. Once they got there, Scott asked the receptionist at the front desk "Hi, is Officer McKinley on duty right now?"

The receptionist shook her head. "Sorry kid. He's not feeling well today. Officer Miles is second in command, so she's the acting police chief today."

Scott looked at Adrian and Erica and shrugged. "Can we talk to her?" he asked.

The receptionist looked at her calendar. "Sure, I don't see why not." She pushed a button on the phone next to her. "Officer Miles to the front desk, please." She gestured to a bench in the waiting area. "You three can wait here. She'll be out in a minute."

The three of them each took a seat on the bench and just as the receptionist had said, a police officer came down shortly.

"Officer Miles. These three are here to see you," the receptionist said, pointing to Adrian, Scott, and Phoebe.

The officer walked over to the three of them and said "I'm Officer Miles. Amelia Miles. What can I help you three with?"

"It's a bit of a sensitive matter; is there somewhere private that we can talk to you?" Scott asked.

"Of course," Officer Miles said, "We can go to my office. Follow me." She led them down that hallway into an office in the corner. "Here, take a seat," she said, gesturing to some seats across from her desk.

She took a seat at her desk and asked "So, what are your names?"

"I'm Scott, this is Adrian, and this is Phoebe," Scott said.

"Oh, you three are the ones who helped us catch that car thief a few months ago. Very impressive, I must say."

"You know about that?" Adrian asked.

"Well, of course. Officer McKinley told me about it. But, if I recall correctly, there was four of you, wasn't there?"

"Well, yes," said Scott. "In fact, that's what we are here to talk to you about."

"Okay, well I am all ears," said Officer Miles. She pulled out a clipboard and a pen. "You don't mind if I take notes, right?"

"Oh, uh, actually, it's probably better if you don't," Scott said. "We don't know who might see those notes."

"I've never had someone make that request before," said Office Miles, surprised. "Now you've gotten me intrigued."

"Don't worry, this will all make sense after I explain it," Scott said. "Let me start at the beginning."

Scott retold what Erica had told him for the second time that day and then explained what they had found at his house. When he was finished, he said "So, now you understand why this has to be kept secret, right?"

Officer Miles slowly nodded her head. "I do..." she said. "Do you happen to know where Erica is right now?"

They all shook their heads. "No, we haven't seen her since lunch period at school," Phoebe said. "And she never tells us where she's going."

"I see. And does Erica know who these two men are?"

"No," Scott said. "She told me that they always wear masks when they are talking to her and she's never seen their actual faces."

"Okay, and you said that you had footage of her breaking into your house," Officer Miles continued. "Do you have it with you?"

"Uh, yes," Scott said, pulling his laptop and the hard drive out of his backpack. He played the video for Officer Miles who watched it curiously.

"These are trained criminals," she said, once the video had finished. "They know how to stay out of view of the camera, but still close enough to grab the things your friend hands out the window."

"So, what can we do without putting Erica in danger?" Phoebe asked.

Officer Miles bit her lip. "We have to get Erica to a safe place, like here, until we can get the tracker off of her. Once we get the tracker off her, the thieves will have no way of tracking her."

"But how are we supposed to talk to her?" Adrian asked. "They can hear everything we say to her."

"I understand that. Which concerns me, since the only ankle monitors that have mics built in are special police-grade ones that no civilian should have access to," Officer Miles said, furrowing her brow. "Which means that they probably worked on the police force for a time, which makes them even more dangerous."

"So, why are they robbing houses, then?" Scott asked. "And why do they need Erica for it?"

"I can't answer your first question," Officer Miles replied. "But as for why they need Erica, I imagine it's easier for them to send someone into the house to collect things, then it is for them to do it themselves. And Erica is fast and agile a.k.a. the perfect person for them. After all, I understand that she is quite the champion at sports in your school."

Officer Miles thought for a second. "Erica still comes to school, correct?" she asked.

"Yes, most of the time," Phoebe said.

"But she leaves in the middle of school sometimes, and we don't see her for the rest of the day," Scott added.

"That's okay," said Officer Miles. "I just need one of you to hand Erica a note asking her to meet you at your parents store where she told you everything the first time."

"Okay..." Scott said, slightly confused.

"Hold on, I'm not done yet," Miles continued. "I'll be there, waiting for her, so I can escort her to the police station where we can find a way to take off the ankle monitor."

"But won't that give the thieves a chance to escape?" Adrian asked. "Once they see that Erica is at the police station, they'll probably make a run for it."

"Mostly likely," Officer Miles agreed. "But right now, the safety of Erica is the most important factor here. We're going to do whatever we can to protect her, even if it means giving the criminals the chance the escape."

"But-," Phoebe started.

Officer Miles held up her hand. "Listen to me. I've been a police officer for over 15 years. I've dealt with cases similar to this one, and in the end, the person in Erica's situation almost always ends up murdered."

The three of them gasped and Adrian asked "Does that mean..."

Officer Miles shook her head. "I promise I'm not going to let that happen to Erica or to any of you. The last thing anybody wants in for a string of robberies to turn into a homicide."

"But why would they kill the person who's doing the work for them?" Scott asked. "That doesn't make any sense."

"Well, in some cases, the hostage tells someone about his or her situation, and the criminals find out, so they kill them. Or sometimes, the criminals rob all the houses they have planned, so they leave town. But first, they kill the hostage so they don't tell anyone about them."

"There's not a lot of expensive houses in this town," Phoebe said. "We might be running out of time!"

"I know," Officer Miles agreed. "That's why I'm asking one of you to give Erica a note rather than one of my officers. It will save time, and she's more likely to listen to you."

Scott nodded. "Okay, I think I can do that. I'll hand her the note before school starts tomorrow morning."

"Make sure you arrive early," said Officer Miles. "You'll want to catch her before any classes start."

Scott nodded again. "Alright, until then, what should be do?" he asked.

"What you normally do," answered Officer Miles. "Homework, chores, and the like. Make sure that you get a lot of rest and don't tell anyone about this."

"What about my parents?" Scott asked.

"I'll send some officers over to their store to clear things up," Officer Miles answered. "Right now, you three should get home. Like I said, just do what you normally do. I will see you three and Erica after school tomorrow, assuming everything goes smoothly."

"Oh, and I almost forgot," she handed them each a card. "If you think of something or something comes up, don't hesitate to give me a call or text."

The three of them took the card and thanked Officer Miles then biked home. On the bike ride home, Scott ran through idea in his head about how he was going to give the note to Erica. Finally, he decided on the simplest idea. He would just hand the note to her before Scott started.

Once he got home, he grabbed a piece of paper and wrote the note:

"Meet me in the warehouse behind my parent's store after school. You'll understand why later."

Scott folded up the note and stuck it in his backpack. He was about to start his homework when he realized something. What happened if the thieves demanded Erica come help them with another robbery the way they had today and Erica couldn't make it to the store.

Scott pulled the card that Officer Miles had handed him and called the number on it. Officer Miles picked up on the second ring.

"Hello, who's this?" she asked.

"Officer Miles, it's Scott. I think there's a problem with your plan to hand Erica a note," Scott said quickly.

"I'm listening, Scott. What's the issue?" Miles asked.

Scott explained the problem that he had thought of. "What do we do then?" he asked.

"You're right," Miles answered. "I didn't think of that. Let me think about this for a minute."

Officer Miles put Scott on hold while Scott impatiently racked his brain for a plan. Finally, after what seemed like an eternity, Officer Miles came back on and said "You need to tell Erica to ignore any demands from the thieves. Tell her to stay in school all day."

"She won't listen to me," said Scott. "She's scared. She's going to do whatever the thieves say."

"No, she won't," Miles responded. "You're her friend, so she'll trust you."

"But-," Scott started.

"No buts," Miles responded. "You need to trust me, Scott. Explain the situation to Erica in a note. Don't say anything, just hand her the note."

"What happens if the thieves come after her in school?" Scott asked.

"They won't," Miles said. "They won't risk going after her in a public place like a school. And once they learn that we know everything, they aren't going to waste time going after Erica. They're just going to leave town which means that Erica will be safe."

"But doesn't that mean they'll get away?" Scott asked.

"It's a possibility," Miles responded. "But we're not going to risk Erica's life to catch them. And remember, criminals always slip up eventually. So, even if we don't catch them now, another police force will."

"Okay, and what happens if Erica leaves school anyway?" Scott said. "What do I do then?"

"If any of you see Erica leave school, you give me a call," Miles said. "I'll send out some officers to find her and bring her to the station. I'm counting on that not being necessary, since it will potentially put her in more danger, but just in case, I'll have a few officer on standby."

"Alright," Scott said. "I'll pass her the note in the parking lot before school starts. Thank you."

"Of course," Miles said. "Just remember, Scott. Be careful. Don't say anything about the note to Erica. Just silently hand it to her and continue on with the school day."

"I think I can do that," said Scott. "Just give me some time to write the note."

"Alright, I will see you tomorrow," Miles said. "Until then, be careful, and have a good evening."

"Thanks," Scott said, hanging up the phone and picking his pencil back up. He pulled the note he had written out of his backpack and crumpled it up. He grabbed another piece of note from his drawer, and started rewriting the note.

"Erica, meet me in the warehouse behind my parent's store after school. You'll understand why later. Ignore any texts from the thieves and stay in school all day."

Scott was about to stick the note back in his bag when he stopped and decided to add something else to the note. Grabbing his pencil again, he wrote:

"We're going to get you out of this mess. Just trust me. You're going to be fine."

Now Scott decided the note was done. He folded it up and stuck it in his bag like he had done with the last one and got started on his homework. He did what Miles had told him, and treated it like any normal day.

As expected, his parents returned home in a panic, after the officers informed them about what had happened. They asked Scott what happened, and Scott said that he come home from school, and he had found it like this. He left out any mention of Erica, not only for her safety, but also for his parent's safety.

Scott went to bed early, after doing all his chores, since Miles had told him to get some rest. Despite lying in bed, though, he simply couldn't fall asleep, so instead, he starting texting Phoebe.

"Hey Phoebe. Are u awake?" he texted.

It took a few minutes, but Phoebe responded with. "Yes, of course. I don't think I'll be able to fall asleep tonight."

"Me neither. What are we going to do if the thieves come after Erica?"

"I don't know," Phoebe texted. "Did you write the note?"

"Yes," Scott replied. "I hope she listens to it."

"She will," Phoebe sent. "Erica might be scared, but she's not going to give up. She wants this to end even more than we do."

"She sounded like she was going to when I talked to her at the store," Scott texted.

"She did?" Phoebe asked.

"Yes, she said that she guessed she was a criminal now and we should try and forget about her," Scott replied.

"I'm sure Erica only said that to try and keep you out of danger," Phoebe sent. "She didn't want you, me, or Adrian getting involved in this."

"Well, we are now," Scott texted. "But what if she actually meant that? What if she's actually giving up?"

"When have you known Erica to give up on something?" Phoebe replied.

"Never, but Officer Miles said that these guys might have been former police officers. That doesn't really stack the odds in our favor."

"Well, thinking like that isn't helping."

"I know, I know. I'm sorry, but I'm just really nervous."

"I am as well and I'm sure Adrian is too. But Erica is going to be fine. Even if the police don't catch the criminals, Erica will be safe and I doubt that they'll come back for Erica, once they learn that the police are looking for them."

"You're right," Scott texted. "Thanks. I really needed and encouraging message like that."

"Of course," Phoebe replied. "Now we need to get some sleep. The average person needs at least 8 and a half hours of sleep, but we should get more to prepare for tomorrow."

"Yeah, I'll see you tomorrow morning," Scott texted, then lay back down in bed. He lay awake for about half an hour, but he was finally able to fall asleep."

Chapter VII

The next morning, Scott, Phoebe, and Adrian all got to school early and met up in the parking lot.

"Alright, do you have the note, Scott?" Phoebe asked.

Scott nodded and pulled the note out of his backpack. "As soon as I see her, I'll slip this note to her."

"Remember, don't say anything out loud," Adrian said. "Just hand her the note."

"I know. I've been running this scenario in my head all last night and this morning," Scott said. "I really hope this works."

"It's going to," said Adrian. "It has to."

"There's still 20 minutes until school starts," Phoebe said. "What should we do while we're here?"

"We can go over the plan again," Adrian suggested.

"No," Scott said quickly. "We've already gone through the plan at least 100 times. We need to find something else to pass the time."

"We can talk about the weekly quiz that out chemistry teacher is going to throw at us today," Adrian said.

"Wait, that's today? Oh no, I am totally going to fail it." Scott asked. "Are you sure it's today?"

"Positive," Adrian said. "It's like clockwork. Mrs. Burke always gives students a quiz on Friday every week. She's been doing it for the last 35 years of her teaching."

"35 years!" Scott said. "Isn't it time for her to retire?"

"Well, I think she likes torturing students with too much homework and quizzes that cover material that we haven't learned yet," Adrian said, laughing.

"I don't know what you're talking about," Phoebe said. "Mrs. Burke's style of teaching is great. Weekly quizzes help cement the material that we just learned into our brains. And I hardly find the amount of homework she gives us, excessive. In fact, she's the only one who gives us enough."

Adrian and Scott started at Phoebe. "You can't possibly believe that," said Scott.

"She assigned us a 3-page essay on defining an element on the 4th day of class," said Adrian. "What teacher does that?"

Phoebe burst out laughing. "I'm joking, I'm joking. Even I think Mrs. Burke gives too much homework. Although the quizzes don't bother me. I actually find quizzes and test to be rather relaxing."

"I didn't know you were capable of joking," said Scott. "You're always so serious."

"Too much homework is an understatement," muttered Adrian. "I stayed up until 3am finishing that stupid report. And then I failed her darn weekly quiz because I was so tired."

"Well, if you paid more attention during class, you wouldn't have failed the exam," Phoebe said.

"Oh no, do not get started on that again," Adrian protested. "Her quizzes aren't even on the things she teaches."

"Guys, Erica is here!" Scott said, gesturing to the parking lot entrance where Erica was walking in.

"Okay, go give her the note," said Adrian.

"Yeah, okay," Scott nodded. He pulled the note out of his pocket and walked over to Erica. Unfortunately for Scott, Erica asked, "Scott, what do you want? I told you to leave me alone."

Scott hadn't thought about what he was going to say if Erica talked to him first. Thinking quickly, he put the note in Erica's hand and put his finger to his lips. He said "I just wanted to know how the soccer game went last night."

Erica looked confused, but she played along and said "It didn't go very well. We lost the game 6 to 0."

"Oh, that stinks," said Scott, gesturing to the note. "Well, we should get inside before the bell rings. Good luck on your next game."

"Yeah, thanks," Erica said, walking into school and unfolding the note that Scott had handed her."

Scott ran back to Adrian and Phoebe and said, "Okay, I think she understood what I was doing. Now we just have to hope that she doesn't leave school at all."

Adrian nodded. "Okay, let's go inside. We can keep an eye on her during classes."

They all went inside and the bell rang shortly after, so they each headed to their classes. Scott and Erica had similar class schedules, so he was able to keep watch on Erica up until the end of P.E.

Scott tried to follow Erica out of P.E. but lost her in the mob of students swarming to lunch. Instead, he found Adrian packing up his gear.

"Do you know where Erica went?" Scott asked.

Adrian looked around. "She's standing in line right there," he said, pointing to a spot on the line. "Phoebe is behind her."

"Wow, you have good eyesight," said Scott. "Let's see if we can meet up with Phoebe after we get our food."

Adrian shoved his gym shirt in his bag and said "Okay, let's go." They took a spot in the back of the line and waited to get their food. Once they got their tray, Scott looked around the cafeteria for Phoebe or Erica.

"Do you see them?" he asked Adrian.

"Phoebe's right there," said Adrian, walking over to a table in the corner. Scott followed him and they set their trays down next to Phoebe.

"I lost sight of Erica after she got her lunch tray," said Phoebe. "I was watching her in line, but I lost her in a crowd of people...wait, there she is."

She pointed to a table in the opposite corner as them, where Erica was sitting and looking at her phone.

"Okay, this is usually when the thieves tell her to leave school and help them with a robbery," Scott said. "I'm hoping she ignore their messages."

They all watched as Erica pulled out Scott's note from her pocket and studied it intently. They could tell that her phone kept going off by the way that she kept instinctively reaching for her pocket, and then pulling her hand back.

"I think that she's ignoring the thieves' messages," said Adrian. "That's good, but she looks really nervous."

"Well, she's never ignored their messages before," said Scott. "I'd be nervous if I was in her position as well."

"What if they come after her at school?" Phoebe asked.

"Officer Miles said that they wouldn't," Scott said. "She said that it was too risky for them to come out in such a public place."

The three of them watched Erica throughout the rest of lunch period, and she didn't leave the cafeteria. Scott watched her throughout the rest of the classes until the final class which only she took.

As soon the bell rang Scott packed up his things and headed to Erica's last class in hopes of catching her before she left the school. Thankfully, Adrian was already on Erica's tail, since his last class ended a few minutes before the bell rang.

Scott followed Adrian and Erica from a distance until they got to the parking lot where they met up with Phoebe.

"Everything seems smooth," said Scott.

"We have a problem," said Phoebe. "We forgot about the walk to your store. The thieves might ambush Erica on her way to your store."

"You're right, I didn't think of that." Scott ran up to Adrian and said "Go talk to Erica and stall her. I need to talk to Officer Miles."

"What's the matter?" Adrian asked.

"Just stall Erica," Scott said. "I'll explain later."

Adrian shrugged and ran over to Erica. Scott grabbed his phone and dialed Officer Miles. She picked up on the first ring and said "Scott, did everything go as planned?"

"Yes, but there's a problem. We're worried that the thieves might try to ambush Erica on her walk to the store, since she's been ignoring their texts," Scott said, as fast as he could.

"I have that covered," said Officer Miles. "I told a few officers to patrol the area between the store and the school. They're keeping an eye on Erica and making sure she gets to the store safely."

"Okay, thank you so much," Scott said. "I'll see you in a bit."

He hung up the phone and signaled to Adrian that he could stop stalling Erica. Phoebe walked over to him and asked, "Did you sort everything out?"

"Officer Miles has it covered," said Scott. "Let's get our bikes."

Adrian ran over to Scott and Phoebe and said "Okay, I stalled her by talking about her the chemistry. Which I'm sure I failed, by the way."

"Thanks," said Scott. "I just wanted to make sure that the thieves didn't try to kidnap Erica on her way to the store. Officer Miles was already thinking ahead, though."

The three of them hopped on their bikes and tore down the streets, heading for the store. Once they got there, they parked their bikes behind the store. Scott unlocked the heavy steel door that led to the store's back room and they walked in.

"Scott, Phoebe, Adrian. Where's Erica?" Officer Miles walked into view from behind a stack of boxes.

"Hi Officer Miles," Scott said. "She's on her way here, I think."

"You think?" Officer Miles asked.

"Well, I assume so," said Scott. "I know she was ignoring the thieves' messages and she was walking in the direction of the store, so..."

The front door suddenly opened and Erica walked in. "Scott, what's going on? You know that I'm basically playing with fire right now, right?"

Scott walked to Erica and said "Don't panic, okay." He gestured for Adrian, Phoebe, and Officer Miles to come forward.

Horrified, Erica said, "You told them!? Why? I told you to forget about me. And why did you call the police? You've basically just signed my death note."

"Erica, it's okay," said Officer Miles. "You're going to be fine. We have a plan, but you just need to trust us."

"No, I-I can't," said Erica. "If they find out that you know about them, they'll kill me and then come for you." Erica looked panicked and nervous and she seemed to be on the verge of tears.

"Erica, listen to me." Phoebe stepped forward and grabbed Erica's hand. "We know you're scared that they're going to kill you, but I promise you, you're going to be fine. We're here to get you out of this mess, but we can't help you if you won't trust us."

"But what about the-the...," Erica's voice broke off and she started to cry.

Phoebe squeezed Erica's hand. "Forget about them. They aren't going to hurt you, and we're going to make sure of it."

"You promise?" Erica asked and Phoebe nodded.

Erica wiped her eyes and hugged Phoebe who hugged her back. "Okay, what do you want me to do?" she asked, standing up straight.

"There's an unmarked police car parked out back," Officer Miles said. "We're going to take you to the police station, where we'll find a way to get the tracker off."

"Wait, but won't they be able to track us in the car?" Scott asked. "Even if we don't say anything?"

"Oh, I have a plan for that," Adrian said, digging around in his bag. He pulled out a roll of aluminum foil. "Blocks all signal," he said.

"That's genius," said Phoebe. "I should've thought of that."

Erica rolled up her pant leg and Adrian wrapped layers of aluminum foil around the tracker. "It might look a little strange, but it will block all signal until we can get it off," he said.

"And how are we going to get it off?" Erica asked. "It's a combination lock with 4 digits and there's no way to cut it off without cutting my leg off."

"I'll explain when we're in the car," Officer Miles said. "We need to get out of here before the thieves figure out where you are."

"Wouldn't it be a good thing if they came here, though?" asked Scott. "Then you could arrest them."

"If my hunch is right, and these criminals used to be cops, there's no way I'm going to be able to arrest them before then manage to shoot all five of us and backup will never arrive in time," Officer Miles said. "I'm confident in my abilities, but not *that* confident. So, let's go now!"

They were all about to rush out the door, when Scott suddenly stopped and asked "What about my parents? What happens if the thieves come and invade the store?"

"I'm pretty sure that's covered already," Erica said. "The store was deserted when I came in."

"Yep, I explained everything to your parents and asked them to shut the store down for the day," Officer Miles replied.

They all ran to the car and Miles hit the gas and drove off to the police station. "Okay, so now that we're on our way, can you tell me how I'm supposed to get this thing of my leg?" Erica asked.

"We have a machine that can run though all the different combinations that the lock has," Miles said. "It can go through a combination in about 5 seconds."

"But there's thousands of combinations," said Erica. "Won't that take days?"

"There's exactly ten thousand different combinations," said Phoebe. "And if the machine can test a combination in 5 seconds, it will take about 13.9 hours to go through all of them."

"14 hours!" Erica said. "What am I supposed to do for those 14 hours?"

"It probably won't take that long," Officer Miles said. "It will only take 14 hours if the last combination the machine tries is the right combination, which would be 9999. It will most likely take around 6-7 hours."

"What do I do for those 7 hours?" Erica asked.

"Read, watch TV, get some rest, basically whatever you want," Miles said. "You just need to relax and let the machine do its job."

"It's really not that bad," Phoebe said. "Remember, I was stuck in a jail cell for almost 2 days, and I survived. It's really boring, though, so at least you'll have access to things, like your phone, books, and other things."

Miles chuckled. "Yeah, McKinley told me about that. I guess it wasn't one of our finest arrests."

Phoebe rolled her eyes as Miles pulled the car up to the police station. "Okay, here we are," she said. She escorted them all out of the car, and walked them inside.

"Officer Wesley, can you set up the combination machine?" Miles asked another officer standing nearby.

"On it, Officer Miles," the officer said, heading off into the back room.

"Okay, so the sooner we get this ankle monitor off you, the better," said Miles to Erica. "But we'll have to take off aluminum foil to let the machine get access to it."

"Won't that give away my location?" Erica asked nervously.

"Yes, but as soon as the thieves realize that you're at a police station, they're going to beat it," Miles said, reassuringly. "Honestly, we'll probably never see them again, unless they get arrested by another police force, which would be a good thing."

"If you're sure," said Erica. She slowly unraveled the aluminum foil from her ankle and asked, "So, where do I go?"

"Officer Wesley is setting up the machine now," said Miles. "For now, you can just sit with your friends and I'll let you know when it's ready."

Erica nodded and took a seat on the bench next to Scott. "Where are Adrian and Phoebe?" she asked.

"Adrian's in the bathroom," said Scott. "And Phoebe is off checking out the machine that they're going to use to guess the combination."

"Sounds like Phoebe," Erica laughed. Then she turned to Scott and said, "Thanks for everything you've done. I appreciate none of you giving up on me."

"Well, we wouldn't be very good friends if we gave up on you, would we?" Scott asked. "And besides, even though you told me that you'd given up, I knew you hadn't."

"Well, for whatever the reasons you had, thank you," Erica said. "I did really think that was going to be my life. Or that they would just kill me and nobody would ever figure out who did it."

"We were never going to let that happen," said Scott. "We all look out for each other."

Officer Miles stepped into the room. "Erica, the machine is ready," she said. "It might take a while, so prepare yourself for a long wait, but if you need anything, I'll be in the office right next door."

Erica got up and followed Officer Miles into a room with a large machine in it. There was a robotic hand mounted to the side of it and it honestly looked rather scary to Erica.

"Here, just take a seat on this chair," said Miles, patting a cushioned, brown chair next to the machine. "There's a TV mounted on the wall in front of you, and I took the liberty of bringing you some books that

Phoebe told me you would like." She pointed to a stack of books next to chair.

Erica thanked Officer Miles and took a seat on the chair and rested her leg on the footstool that was in front of the chair.

"Okay, start it up, Officer Wesley," Miles called out. There was a whirring sound, and suddenly the machine jolted to life. The claw hand moved towards the ankle monitor on Erica's leg and started spinning the dials at super speed.

"It'll keep doing this until it hits the right combination," Miles said. "Until then, just relax. The worst is behind you."

Erica smiled and grabbed a book off the stack. "I'm sure it'll be over before I even know it," she said.

"Oh, I almost forgot," Miles said. "I hate to do this to you, but if you could, can you give us a description of the two men who kidnapped you? It doesn't need to be too detailed; just whatever you can remember."

Erica thought for a bit. "They were always wearing masks when they talked to me, so I'm not entirely sure, but I think one of them had blue eyes. They were both very big, but not tall. Oh, and one was always wearing white sneakers. There might be more, but I'm not Phoebe, so I can't remember that many details."

"No, that's perfectly okay. You've been through a lot, and I don't expect you to have their facial features and body type perfectly memorized. What you gave me is plenty."

Officer Miles left the room and walked out to where Adrian, Scott, and Phoebe were sitting. "You three can go home now," she said. "Erica will be back at school tomorrow and you three should probably get your homework done. Thanks for all your help. Me and the rest of the police force really appreciate it and I'm sure Erica does as well."

"And you're sure that the two men who kidnapped Erica won't come back," asked Adrian.

"Almost positive," Miles responded. "I've got some officers out looking for them now, but they've probably already left town. This is most likely the last we'll ever see of them."

"Well, thank you, Officer Miles," said Scott. He shook her hand. "We'll probably drop in a few times just to see how Erica is doing," he said.

The three of them said bye to Erica and left the police station. They each headed home and were finally able to start on their homework and get their chores done. They each occasionally popped in to say "hi" to Erica, and by the time nighttime came, they were all ready to fall asleep.

In fact, both Scott and Phoebe were finally able to get a good night's sleep, no longer worrying about what was happening to Erica, or potentially fearing for their lives.

Chapter VIII

The next morning, they all met in the school parking lot, including Erica this time, minus the ankle monitor.

"So, what did the combination end up being?" Scott asked.

"I think it was 8673," said Erica. "I have no idea why they picked those four numbers, but it certainly took long enough for it to finally unlock."

Adrian chuckled. "Well, at least this is all behind us now," he said. "We can forget about it and go on with our lives."

Erica winced. "I don't think I'll ever be able to forget about this," she said. "It's the kind of thing that stays with you for the rest of your life." She looked at Scott. "You know, it's kind of like being kidnapped and tortured," she said.

"You're referring to the car thief?" Scott asked. Erica nodded. "I still think about that every week." She shuddered and looked at Adrian. "You got lucky. You have no idea how painful those electric shocks were."

"You're right," said Adrian. "But at least you got to watch them getting what they deserved."

"That's what makes this whole thing even worse," Erica said. "Look what they did to me." She rolled up her sweater sleeve to reveal a long scar that looked to be caused by a knife. Phoebe and Adrian winced.

"They did that to me when I told them I wasn't going to help them rob Scott's house," Erica said, pulling her sweater down. "And they're just going to get away with everything. Plus, they get to keep everything they stole with no repercussions."

"But you're safe," said Phoebe. "And not to sound cliché, but isn't that what matters."

"It is," Erica agreed. "But am I really safe? I'm always going to keep looking around me and worrying that someday they're going to come back for me or that someone else is going to come and do the same thing to me. I don't think I'll ever feel better until I know that they're either in jail for life or dead."

Scott raised his eyebrows. "Dead," he asked. "Isn't that a bit much?"

"Sure, but at least I'll know that they can't hurt me," said Erica. The school bell started to ring and Erica sighed. "Might as well get to class, I guess," she said and headed out of the parking lot. The rest of them watched her and Adrian said, "This is terrible. She's never going to feel better until the thieves are caught."

"I know," said Scott. "But what can we do? It's not like we can catch the guys if the police can't."

"I don't know. We can at least try to help her through this," Adrian said, as the second bell rang. "We should go before we're late."

"I'll see if I can think of something," said Phoebe, walking into school. "I'm sure there's something that we can do."

Scott and Adrian followed Phoebe into school, all of them trying to think of what they could do to help Erica.

Later, at lunch period, all four of them got their lunch and took a seat at their usual table. Scott set his tray down on the table and said to Erica, "Hey, thanks for not taking any of my stuff from the house. You left my computer and stereo alone."

"I only took what they could see from the windows," said Erica. "I didn't want to help them take anything, so I just took the bare minimum to please them."

"Didn't they know that you'd be on video?" Adrian asked.

"Well, yeah, but they didn't care," said Erica. "As long as nobody saw them, they were okay throwing me under the bus." She put her fork down. "Look, can we talk about something else?" she asked. "I'm trying to forget about this, even though I probably never will."

"Of course, sorry," said Scott. "There's a soccer game today, isn't there?"

Erica nodded silently, and stared at the table, not saying anything. "Erica, are you okay?" Phoebe asked.

"I don't know, I guess," said Erica. "It's just that I keep expecting my phone to go off and for them to demand that I do another job for them. Even though I tossed out that phone, since they bugged it and did who knows what else with it."

"I have an idea," said Scott. "Do you remember that discussion we had in the music room a few months ago?" he asked.

"Vaguely," Erica responded, looking up. "Why? You're not thinking of starting-." She trailed off. "Actually, it might not be a bad idea."

"Starting what?" asked Phoebe and Adrian. "If you could fill us in, that would be great," said Adrian.

"A band," said Scott. "A few months ago, Erica and I talked about the four of us starting a band. Me playing guitar, Erica playing the drums, Phoebe playing the keyboard, and well, we hadn't decided what Adrian could do yet."

"Wait, a band?" asked Adrian. "Where did that come from?"

"Well, we all like playing instruments, and we've gotten pretty good at it over the years," said Scott. "So, we might as well consider starting a band. Would you guys be up for it?"

"Sure!" said Phoebe. "I've been meaning to try something new, anyway, and it'll be a nice way to get my mind off of STEM and the PSAT all the time."

"Yeah, and it'll help Erica forget about what happened to her," said Scott. He looked at Erica. "It'll give you something to focus your mind on and help prevent you from thinking about you know what all the time."

"Well, I guess it can't hurt to give it a try," said Erica. "But what about Adrian?"

Scott turned to Adrian. "Can you play any instruments?" he asked.

"Are you crazy?" Adrian said excitedly. "I've played the bass since I was 10. You didn't know?"

Scott looked at him, surprised. "Seriously? You've never mentioned that even once," he said. "I had no idea."

Adrian shrugged. "Well, now you do, I guess. And I think starting a band is a great idea. The bass doesn't sound very good on its own."

"Well, then it's settled," Scott said. "We can meet tomorrow after school in the music room and discuss how we want to do this."

"Why tomorrow?" asked Erica. "Why not today?"

"Oh, I have a dentist's appointment after school," Scott replied. "But we're all free tomorrow, right?"

Everyone nodded, and Scott said "Great! Don't forget to bring your instruments to school tomorrow."

The bell rang and they all dumped their trays in the trash and headed for their respective classrooms, looking forward to getting the band started tomorrow.

After school, like always, the four of them met in the parking lot and discussed what they were going to do later today.

"Well, after my dentist appointment, which always takes 2 hours longer than it's supposed to, I won't have time for much else other than homework," Scott said. "So, I'll probably be stuck home all day."

"Yeah, I have another science project to work on," said Phoebe. "But other than that, I don't have much else to do."

"You always have a science project to do," Adrian joked. "You should take a break sometimes."

"What, no!" Phoebe said, offended. "I need to win the tournament, but every time I think I have the perfect project, I think of something better."

Erica laughed, for the first time in days. "I'll just hang around the park," she said. "Shoot some hoops, try to take my mind off of everything and get back to a normal schedule."

"And I have to tutor Katie, because of course I do," said Adrian. "She seems to be unable to grasp the knowledge of basic addition."

"Well, you know, I could tutor her," Phoebe suggested. "I don't have much else to do."

"No!" said Adrian hastily. "Sorry Phoebe, while you are the smartest person I know, you'd make an awful tutor."

"I would not," Phoebe said indignantly. "What on earth makes you think that?"

"Adrian's sorta right," said Scott. "I mean, come on, Phoebe. You have no patience for people not understanding things. You'd get frustrated with Katie so easily. Trust me, I know, because I tried to tutor her once."

"Yeah, and you vowed to never do it again," said Adrian. "You said, and I quote, 'I would rather walk over a bed of burning hot nails in bare feet then do that again.'"

"Well...I might have exaggerated a bit, but I feel sorry for you," said Scott. "But let's stop discussing why we hate tutoring Katie and discuss our band plans." Scott checked his watch, and his eyes grew wide. "Shoot! I've gotta be home in 3 minutes," he said. He ran to his bike and tore off. "See you guys tomorrow!" he yelled and waved.

"Yeah, we should all get home," Erica said. "Anyone want to come with me to the basketball court?"

Adrian shook his head. "Sorry Erica. Mom will have a fit if I'm late to tutor Katie." He rolled his eyes. "And that usually means I end up having to tutor Katie even more." He pulled his bike off the bike rack and said "See you guys tomorrow."

Erica looked at Phoebe and said, "Pretty sure I already know your answer."

Phoebe shrugged. "Sorry, as you well know, sports aren't my thing. Now, if you had a math problem that needed to be solved, then sure!"

"Alright, well, see you tomorrow, I guess," said Erica. "I'm sure there's someone at the park who will want to shoot hoops with me."

Phoebe waved goodbye and headed home on foot, while Erica headed to the park, which was only a couple blocks away.

Chapter IX

About half an hour later, Phoebe was downstairs spreading jam on toast when there was a pounding at the front door. Unsure of who could be at the door, Phoebe put her toast down and walked to the door. She opened it, and Erica, looking distraught and panicked ran into the house.

"Erica, what's going?" Phoebe asked. "What's the matter?"

"They're back again!" Erica said. "The two men who kidnapped me; I saw them at the basketball court, watching me."

Phoebe instantly shut and locked the door. "Are you sure it was them?" she asked.

"Yes, I'm sure!" Erica said. "They were wearing the same masks as before. They're coming to kill me!"

"So, did they see you come in here?" Phoebe asked Erica.

Erica shrugged. "I don't know, but I hope not," she said. "What am I supposed to do now?"

"Alright, let me call Officer Miles," said Phoebe. "I'll let her know that the thieves haven't left town and that we're in my house."

Phoebe picked up the phone and dialed Officer Miles who picked up the phone and said "Phoebe! What can I do for you?"

Phoebe got straight to the point and said, "The thieves are back. Erica says she saw them while playing basketball in the park."

"Okay, where are you right now?" Miles asked. "I'll come over and bring you two to the police station."

"We're at my house," Phoebe responded.

"Alright, and do the thieves know that Erica is there?" Miles asked.

"I don't know," said Phoebe. "She might have been followed, but she's not sure."

"Okay, I will be there in a few minutes. Sit tight, and stay away from windows. And of course, don't open the door unless you hear my voice." Miles hung up, leaving Phoebe and Erica trying to regain their wits.

"Are you okay?" Phoebe asked Erica, who was sitting on the couch, looking anxiously around.

"Mentally or physically?" Erica asked. "Officer Miles assured me that they would leave town and I'd never have to see them again."

"Sometimes people make mistakes," said Phoebe. "These men must be really desperate if they'd risk being caught by the police in order to catch you."

"That's not comforting at all," muttered Erica. "That basically means I'm being hunted by two desperate men trying to get revenge on me for reporting them."

"Well, look on the bright side," Phoebe said, trying to encourage Erica. "Since they're desperate, it means that they'll probably be more likely to slip up and give themselves away."

"Sure, or they'll be more careful," Erica said. "I'm done for. I knew should have never told Scott anything. I should have just kept doing what they told me to."

"Hey, don't think like that," said Phoebe. "I'm sure Officer Miles has a plan, and nobody is going to let anything happen to you."

"Phoebe, Erica?" Officer Miles asked from outside. "Are you two in there?"

Phoebe walked over to the door and opened it. "Officer Miles, what do we do?"

"The police car is parked right outside," Miles responded. "I canvassed the area, but I didn't see anybody, so I think we're safe." She looked Erica. "I'm really sorry I told you that they would leave town. In most cases like this, the criminals don't bother going after the hostage after they tell the police."

Erica got up off the couch. "They aren't going to stop until they kill me, are they?" she asked.

Officer Miles nodded. "I'm afraid that is most likely the case. Which is why we are doing everything to can to catch them," she added quickly.

"I've heard that before," said Erica. "And then the criminals never get caught."

"I'm sorry Erica," Officer Miles said. "I can't promise you that we'll catch the criminals, but I can promise you that we'll make sure we keep you safe."

Erica sighed and followed Officer Miles and Phoebe to the car outside. Miles drove to the police station and when they got there she said, "Erica, I think it's best if you stay here, since the criminals know where you live."

"What about the rest of my family?" Erica asked. "Won't they be in danger if they stay in the house?"

"I'll have Officer Harris explain everything to them and bring them to a safehouse a few blocks away from the police station," Miles responded. "Since the thieves aren't hunting for them, as long as they stay away from the house, they should be safe."

"Wait, you have safehouses in this town?" Phoebe asked. "Where?"

"We have multiple safehouses throughout the town," said Miles. "They're basically just non-descript houses with lots of emergency exits built in. Unfortunately, I can't tell you where they are, since that would compromise the security of them."

She looked around the police station and said to Erica, "You should be safe here. I'll make sure there's an officer outside at all times, even during lunch break and nighttime. If nobody can do it, I'll do it myself," she said. "Right now, our priority is on finding out information on these two men and figuring out where they might be hiding."

"Officer Miles. I might have something that could be useful," said Phoebe.

Miles raised her eyebrows. "I'm listening," she said.

"So, a few days ago, and man came to my house asking for Erica. I told them that I didn't know who she was, but I think that man might be affiliated with the two thieves who kidnapped Erica," Phoebe said.

"It's a lead," said Miles. "Do you remember anything about the man?"

"Of course," said Phoebe. "Photographic memory and all. He was tall, probably about 6ft, had dirty blonde, curly hair and a short beard. He was wearing a sweatshirt with the Bears logo on it, and ripped jeans."

"That sounds like Hubert Pickens," said Miles. "He runs the pawn shop a few blocks down. He's also a known purchasing of stolen goods, so he might be connected to the two men somehow. I'll have a talk with him. In the meantime, Officer Wesley will watch Erica and make sure she's safe."

"Can I come with you to talk to the pawn shop owner?" asked Phoebe. "I could identify him and tell you if it's the same man who came to my house."

Miles shrugged. "I suppose so," she said. "It could prove useful." She gestured for Phoebe to follow her outside to the car, which Phoebe did, and they drove off.

"So, when we get there, be careful," said Miles. "Pickens isn't dangerous, but there's some pretty seedy people who hang out at pawn shops."

"I've been there before," said Phoebe. "My dad was looking for a watch for my uncle's birthday, so he checked the pawn shop. He didn't buy anything though."

"Probably for the best," Miles said, pulling up in front of the pawn shop. The pawn shop was open, so she walked in and the bells on the door jingled.

Miles pointed to the man sitting at the front counter inspecting a gold coin and asked Phoebe. "Does he match the person who came to your door?"

Phoebe took a good look at the man and nodded. "That's him, alright," she said.

"Perfect," said Miles, walking over to the man. She rapped on the counter and the man jumped up. "This is a perfectly legal business," he said, as soon as he saw Miles' uniform.

"Uh-huh, sure it is," said Miles. "We're not here about that, though. You went to a house on Washington St. and asked for an Erica Feldman about three days ago. We're here to find out why."

"No idea what you're talking about," Pickens muttered. "I don't know anybody named Erica."

"Oh please," said Miles. "You and I both know that your pawn shop isn't "perfectly legal". You sell stolen goods all the time."

"Lies," said Pickens. "Everything here was obtained legally."

Phoebe tapped Miles on the shoulder and pointed to a TV that was standing in a corner. "That's Scott's TV," she said. "I recognize it. It was stolen when the thieves forced Erica to rob Scott's house."

"Well, would you look at that," said Miles. "Your "perfectly legal" pawn shop is starting to look a little less "legal" and more "criminal"."

"Woah, hey," Pickens interjected. "That TV belonged to my cousin. He pawned it so he could afford a down payment on a new car."

"Well, we can verify that," said Phoebe. She said to Miles, "Scott told me that he scratched his and Greg's name into the back of the TV when he was 10."

Miles walked over to the TV and turned it around. "Hey, be careful with that," said Pickens. "I can easily get a few hundred for that."

"Or, you can get a few years in jail," Miles said, holding up the TV to show the very clear scratch marks on the back. "You now have two options here, Pickens. Either I arrest you for selling stolen goods and you spend a few years in jail and lose your license to run a pawn shop, or you spill where you got this TV and the rest of your "perfectly legal" items from and I send some officers to collect the stolen goods and we forget this ever happened."

"Okay, okay, chill," Pickens said. "I can't lose my license, and I sure can't go back to jail. That place is the worst."

"So, you'd better starting spilling," said Miles. "I don't have all day."

"Alright man, just don't arrest me," Pickens said. "I get all my stuff from two guys. They usually gave me a location to dump cash they give me a place to go to get the stuff I buy."

"What are the names of the two guys?" Miles asked.

Pickens shrugged. "I dunno. They never told me and I never asked. Didn't need to know, didn't want to know."

"And why were you looking for Erica?" Miles asked.

"Well, the two guys sent me a text telling them that they had a new deliveryman, so if I couldn't find my stuff where it was supposed to be, to go to an address and ask for an Erica Feldman," Pickens said. "I couldn't remember the address, though. It was 250 something and some president's name street. Lincoln, Washington, something like that."

"You said that the thieves sent you a text," said Miles. "I'm going to need your phone to trace the text."

"Woah, hey, you can't take my phone!" Pickens protested. "I need that to-to-"

"To buy stolen goods?" Miles asked, raising her eyebrows. "Give me the phone or I'm arresting you for both impeding an investigation and knowingly purchasing stolen goods."

"Geez, okay," said Pickens, reaching under his desk. He pulled out a cell phone and slapped it on the counter. "Take it, man. Just, can you bring it back to me when you're done."

Miles rolled her eyes and lead Phoebe back out to the car. Once they were in the car, Phoebe said, "His story makes sense. I live on 253 Washington Street and Erica lives on 257 Adams Rd."

"He's an idiot, though," said Miles. "If he really couldn't remember the address, he could have just checked his texts." She was scrolling through his phone's texts and stopped at a conversation with a random number. "Here's the conversation. Now we just need to figure out what cell tower these texts were sent from."

"Won't that only give us a very vague location?" asked Phoebe.

"Sure, but it's better than nothing," Miles replied, driving back to the police station. "It's our first lead, since these criminals have done a pretty good job of covering their tracks." She pulled up at Phoebe's house. "You should go home now," she said. "I'll make sure that Erica's okay, and feel free to drop in whenever you want."

"Okay, thanks for everything," Phoebe said, getting out of the car. "If there's anything I can do to help you catch the thieves, I'd be happy to help."

"You've helped plenty," said Miles. "And, like I said, I can't promise that we're going to catch the criminals, but we will put everything we've got into catching them."

Phoebe thanked Officer Miles again and headed inside, where she called Scott and Adrian to let them know about everything that had just happened.

"Wow, are you sure?" asked Scott. "Officer Miles said that they would leave town."

"That's what I said," said Phoebe. "But Erica swore that she saw them."

"Is she okay?" Adrian asked.

"She's at the police station now," said Phoebe. "Officer Miles said that there would always be an officer watching her and making sure she was safe."

"I'll come visit her after my dentist appointment," said Scott. "Which should be in about an hour."

"And I'll come visit her after my mom says that I'm done tutoring Katie," said Adrian. "Which could be anywhere between 30 minutes and 5 hours."

"Adrian, come here and help me solve this math problem," Katie's voice came over the phone and Adrian sighed. "I'll be there in a second," he called. To Phoebe and Scott, he said, "I've gotta go. We can all go drop in at the police station together at around 6 today. That work for you guys?"

"Yep," said Phoebe and Scott together. "I'll see you then," Scott said. "I'm up next with the dentist."

Chapter X

5 o clock rolled around shortly and they all met up at the corner of Wood St. and Wilson St. They all headed to the police station on their bikes, biking in single file.

Once they got there, Scott opened the door, expecting to find the receptionist there, but surprisingly, there was nobody at the front desk.

"That makes sense," said Phoebe. "The police officers only work at the office from 9-6, and after that, they only take emergency calls."

"So, where's Erica?" Adrian.

"Not sure, but I'm sure somebody's here," Phoebe said. "Officer Miles said that someone would always be keeping watch on Erica."

"Well, Miles' office is down that way," said Scott. "Let's try there."

The three of them walked down the hallway to Officer Miles' office, but she wasn't there. Unsure of what to do next, Phoebe poked her head in the next room over and gasped.

Officer Miles was lying face down on the floor with blood dripping out from a cut on her head. Phoebe rushed over to her and gestured for the rest of them to come over. Phoebe raised Miles' head and felt the cut on the back of her head.

She was unconscious, but breathing, and she clearly had been hit hard on the head with something heavy, like a baseball bat.

"Where's Erica?" Scott asked suddenly.

Almost on queue, there was a scream from outside that sounded like "Help!". They all rushed to the window, but instead of seeing Erica, they saw a green sedan pull out and drive off.

"Erica has to be in there," said Adrian. "What do we do? Police will never get here in time."

Phoebe looked at Officer Miles, but it was clear that she wasn't in any condition to help. She looked at Scott and asked, "You can drive, right?"

"Yes, why?" asked Scott.

"Well, let's go then," she said, grabbing Officer Miles' car key from her pocket. "Her car was parked outside." Phoebe took off towards the exit and yelled to Adrian, "Call 911! Tell them that Erica is in a green sedan and we're following them in a police car."

"Wait, what?" asked Scott chasing after Phoebe. Phoebe threw open the front doors and ran to the police car out front as the green sedan blew past them in the parking lot.

Phoebe pulled the door open and yelled, "Scott, get in the driver's seat!"

"You want me to drive this?" Scott asked. "I- "

"Hurry!" Phoebe yelled, as Adrian jumped into the backseat.

Not sure of what else to do, Scott climbed into the front seat and turned the key in the ignition. The car started up and Scott said, "Here goes nothing." He threw the car into drive and slammed on the gas. The car shot forward and Scott pulled it out onto the road, trying to catch up to the green car who was a few hundred feet in front of them.

"This is crazy!" Adrian said. "Scott doesn't even have a license, and this is a cop car."

"Well, if we waited for the actual police to show up, we'd have lost Erica!" Phoebe said. "Our only hope is to follow them and figure out where they take-woah!" Phoebe bounced around in her seat as Scott made a sharp right turn.

"Hang on tight," said Scott, trying to keep the green car in his vision. He floored the gas pedal and the car zoomed forward, making them all hit the backs of their seats, hard. The green car turned off the main road and Scott followed them, nearly hitting a sign post.

Scott drove down a narrow back road and tried to keep up with green sedan's crazy driving. "Scott, watch out!" Phoebe yelled, and Scott turned the wheel sharply to avoid hitting a mailbox.

"I'm never going to catch them," said Scott. He made another sharp turn, this time out of the backroads, and onto a main road.

"There's an intersection with a red light coming up," said Adrian. "They-never mind." They watched as the car blew right through the red light.

"Scott, you can't make that!" Phoebe exclaimed, watching the cars going east approach in the intersection. "You're going to hit one of them!"

"Not necessarily," Scott said, hitting a button on the dashboard. The lights and sirens on the police car turned on and they watched as all the cars starting hitting their brakes for Scott.

Scott drove through the red light, keeping pace with the green sedan, but suddenly it drove off the main road and onto another backroad. Scott turned along with the car, but as soon as he did, he realized that the road almost instantly led to an intersection with two roads going left and right.

"Which one?" Scott asked, slamming on the brakes and turning off the siren and lights.

"Unsure of what else to do, Phoebe pointed left, and Scott drove the car down the left road. They didn't see the green sedan, though. However, what they did see was a large, abandoned-looking warehouse.

"Why's it always warehouses?" moaned Adrian. "Why can't criminals pick something like a donut shop to be their hideout?"

"Look," Phoebe said, pointing to something near the side of the house. "It's the car. This is definitely the place."

Scott shut the engine off and got out of the car. "So, now what?" he whispered to Phoebe and Adrian.

Adrian and Phoebe got out of the car and Adrian pointed to an open window on the side of warehouse. "Let's see if we can climb in through there," he whispered.

They all crept over to the window and Scott slid it open and they all climbed through the window. They tiptoed around the warehouse, but it was dark and dusty, so there wasn't much they could see.

Suddenly Phoebe stopped walking and put her finger to her lips. They all listened carefully, and they hear a man's voice talking. They couldn't tell what he was saying, but they were able to follow the sound of his voice to locate him.

Eventually, they got close enough to him to hear what he was saying. "You knew what would happen if you went to the police." Then they could hear Erica saying "No, I didn't, I didn't, I swear. They found out from the security footage."

Silently, Scott gestured to the two men standing about 20 feet away from them, but he couldn't see Erica. She was blocked from a view by a large pillar, so Phoebe and Adrian moved closer. Unfortunately, they weren't looking very closely were they were walking, and Adrian accidently kicked a tin can, causing it to rattle.

One of the men looked around and said "Did you hear that?" The other man nodded and grabbed what Scott assumed was a gun from his side, but it was too dark to be sure. They started walking over to where Scott, Adrian and Phoebe were hiding and Scott's heart started to race.

Suddenly, he felt Phoebe pulling on his arm. He turned to her and she silently pointed to a large stack of 2x4's in a corner. Softly and quietly, they all made their way behind the pile and crouched down while the men looked around.

Finally, one of them shrugged and said "Probably just rats." They walked away and Scott, Adrian, and Phoebe all took a deep breath. From this vantage point, they could see both Erica and the men.

Erica was tied to a chair with zip ties, and she looked terrified. One of the men walked over to her and said "We're not here to kill you, just yet. Had we wanted to, we would have done so in the car. We still need you for one more job."

"I already did everything you asked," Erica pleaded. "Why can't you just let me go now. Find somebody else to commit your crimes for you."

"Oh, we will," said the other man. "It's just that this job is perfect for you. So, what do you say? One last robbery before you die?"

"Forget it," Erica said defiantly. "I'm done committing crimes for you. If you're going to kill me no matter what, you might as well get it over with."

"You're sure about that?" the man asked, raising his gun. "It's still another few hours alive, no matter what you're doing."

"Positive," said Erica. "And you know what? Killing me doesn't benefit you. It's just going to make your sentence even longer."

The man chuckled. "Sentence. Ha! That only matters if they catch us."

"Oh, they will," said Erica. "You brought that upon yourself. If you had just given up and left town after the police found out about me, you would've had a chance at escaping, but instead, you *had* to hunt me down."

"Well, it's going to be a bit of a challenge for them to catch us without their star witness," the man said raising his gun to Erica's head.

"Noooooo!" Phoebe yelled, charging out from behind the stack of wood, brandishing a 2x4 like a weapon. She caught the men by surprise, and instead of shooting at Erica the man whirled around and fired his gun at Phoebe.

Phoebe ducked and swung the 2x4 at the man holding the gun. The man dodged it, but Scott and Adrian came running at them, both holding steel pipes.

"Well, look who came to party!" one of the men said. "The more the merrier, I always says."

"You and Adrian take the one with the gun," Scott yelled. "I'll take the other one." He swung the pipe at the man, but instead of ducking or dodging, the man instead grabbed the poll and shoved it back into Scott, knocking the wind out of him.

Meanwhile, Adrian and Phoebe charged at the man with the gun, but he dodged both their swings and kicked Adrian in the stomach, while grabbing Phoebe by her arm and swinging her to the ground.

In short, the fight was very one-sided. It took approximately five minutes for the two men to take down Phoebe, Scott, and Adrian and another five minutes to tie them to chairs next to Erica.

"Now then, where were we before we so rudely interrupted?" the man holding the gun asked. "Oh, that's right." He pointed the gun at Erica's forehead and said "Well, this will be the last thing any of you see."

He squeezed the trigger as the rest of the watched in horror, but unable to do anything. Right before he let go, however, Erica swung backwards in her chair and kicked the man in the shins, hard, causing his hand to move and fire the gun directly above Erica's head, into the heating duct above.

Annoyed, the man rubbed his shin and said "Well, at least you still have some fight in you. Let's try this again, shall we." He raised the gun for the third time, but this time, instead of kicking the man in the shins, Erica swung the chair all the way back, landing it on its edge. This broke the chair's arm, which freed Erica's left hand.

The man was about to fire the gun at Erica on the ground, but Erica swung the chair, which was still zip-tied to her arm, at the man's legs. This knocked the man's legs out from under him, which caused him to fall to the ground and also snapped the zip-tie that was holding Erica's arm to the chair.

The other man charged at Erica, trying grab her, but Erica, now free of restraints, jabbed a piece of wood from the chair into the man's stomach, causing him to double over in pain. The man holding the gun got to his feet, but before he could use his gun, Erica grabbed a metal pipe and feinted a swing to his head, causing the man to instinctively duck, but instead, smashed the pipe into his wrist, making the man drop his gun.

Clutching his wrist, the man scrambled the pick the gun up, Erica beat him to it. She grabbed the gun off the floor, pointed it at the two men, and said "Get up against that wall now!"

The two men raised their hands in defeat, one still clutching his wrist, and walked over to the wall. "Don't shoot, don't shoot," the man said. "We give up." Keeping her eyes on the men, Erica picked up the steel pole from the ground and said:

"This has been a long time coming!"

She grabbed the pole and conked the two men on the head with it, knocking them out.

Using a broken bottle, Erica freed Scott, Adrian, and Phoebe from the chairs, and Scott said "That was impressive," said Scott. "They beat all three of us, and you were able to take down both of them by yourself."

Erica shrugged. "Well, adrenaline, and the fact that I was sick of listening to them and being terrified of them all the time." She looked at the two men, collapsed on the floor and said, "I think I should have hit them harder."

Suddenly, the door burst open and Officer Wesley yelled "Police freeze!"

Erica laughed and called "We're okay! But you might want to do something with these two numbskulls."

Officer Miles came into view. She had a bandage wrapped around the back of her head, but she seemed perfectly fine. "Thank goodness you four are okay," she said.

"Well, thanks to Erica's amazing fighting skills, we are," said Adrian. "She took out both of those men singlehandedly."

"You did?" asked Officer Miles. "That's impressive. It takes a lot to take out two fully-grown men. Especially if their holding a weapon and used to be former police officers."

"Well, what can I say," said Erica. "I took gymnastics when I was younger, and I used to get into fights on the baseball field all the time."

"Hey, how did you know where to find us?" asked Scott. "We're basically in the middle of nowhere."

"Well, you did steal a police car," said Miles. "You don't think we equip every car with a tracking device."

"Oh, yeah," said Scott. "Are we in trouble for that...?"

Miles laughed, "No, of course not. Although, if you do it for any reason other than saving someone's life, it is a federal crime."

"That's not part of the law," said Phoebe. "It just says-"

"It's a joke, Phoebe," Adrian said. "But at least all of this is finally over." They all watched as the officer handcuffed the two groggy men, and shoved them into the police car.

"And I can finally go back to doing what I was doing before," said Erica. "No more constant terror that I'm about to be grabbed again, and no more constant fear that I'm being watched." She rubbed a cut on her arm. "You know, hitting someone you hate on the head with a pole is very therapeutic."

"Well, I suppose that's one way," said Miles. She led the group back outside. "It's time for you guys to go home. And if you ever need anything, don't hesitate to call me."

"Is your head okay?" Scott asked, looking at the bandage on the back of Miles' head.

"Oh, yeah," said Miles. "They just hit me with a baseball bat when I wasn't looking. It's nothing. I've been through much worse."

"Thanks for everything," said Erica. "You're one of the best police officers in this town. You should be police of chief instead of Officer McKinley."

"Woah, don't let him hear you say that," Miles said, getting into the police car. "He'd be pretty offended."

She started the car and drove each of them to their home, where they were more than happy to go. They all waved goodbye and hoped that the rest of the school year wouldn't be quite so adventurous.

"NO, NOT AN E MAJOR chord, an E minor chord," Scott said. The four of them were sitting in the school music room, trying to learn a song to start their band, but it wasn't going so well.

"Erica, your timing is all off," Scott said. "And Adrian, you need to play your bass louder. I can't hear it over my guitar and Erica's drums."

"Hey, why are you in charge?" Phoebe protested. "You're not the best player here."

"I'm just trying to get us to learn a song," said Scott. "If you want to be in charge, be my guest."

"Well, it will have to wait until tomorrow," said Erica, checking her phone. "It's time for me and Scott's fencing lessons."

"Wait, that's today?" Scott asked. "Do I have to go?"

"Hey, you promised!" Erica said. "So, yes, you have to go."

"Alright, fine," Scott said, packing up his guitar. "I'll see you guys tomorrow."

Things were finally back to normal. They hung out as a group again, they told embarrassing stories about each other, and all-in-all, spent time the way they had before. And the events from prior were pushed to the back of everybody's mind, hopefully to never be brought back to the front again.

The End

———————————————

Don't miss out!

Visit the website below and you can sign up to receive emails whenever Travis Cramer publishes a new book. There's no charge and no obligation.

https://books2read.com/r/B-A-CVTIB-TAVQD

BOOKS 2 READ

Connecting independent readers to independent writers.

Did you love *Secrets, Suspicions, and Silence*? Then you should read *Revenge, Rescue, and Revelations*[1] by Travis Cramer!

[2]

Get ready for an exhilarating ride in "Revenge, Rescue, and Revelations," the thrilling third installment of the Misadventure and Mystery series. This time, the stakes are higher, the mysteries deeper, and the adventures more captivating than ever. Join Erica, Adrian, Phoebe, and Scott as they navigate unexpected challenges, unravel secrets, and face dangers head-on.

In this gripping sequel, the team finds themselves entangled in a complex web of lies, deceit, and hidden truths. Their latest quest leads them to uncover dark secrets from the past that threaten to unravel everything they thought they knew. As they delve deeper into the mystery, they encounter formidable foes who will stop at nothing to

---

1. https://books2read.com/u/bwgpKv

2. https://books2read.com/u/bwgpKv

protect their secrets. With unexpected allies appearing in the most unlikely places, the team must rely on their wits, courage, and each other to survive.

Erica's relentless determination, Adrian's strategic mind, Phoebe's keen intuition, and Scott's unyielding loyalty are put to the ultimate test as they face personal demons and external threats. Each twist and turn brings them closer to a revelation that could change everything. Their journey takes them from eerie abandoned buildings to shadowy forests, and from high-stakes confrontations to heart-pounding escapes.

Amidst the action and suspense, the characters' relationships deepen, and their individual stories unfold in poignant and surprising ways. The bonds they share are tested as they confront betrayal, danger, and the daunting task of uncovering the truth. With heart-pounding action, intricate plotlines, and unforgettable characters, "Revenge, Rescue, and Revelations" will keep you on the edge of your seat from start to finish. Will the team uncover the truth and save the day, or will the forces against them prove too powerful? Dive into this electrifying adventure and find out in a story that promises to captivate, surprise, and entertain. This book is not just a continuation of the series, but a deepening of the saga that fans have come to love. Prepare for a journey that will leave you breathless and eager for more.

Read more at https://books2read.com/ap/81Do3O/ Travis-Cramer.

Also by Travis Cramer

Misadventure and Mystery
Cars, Computers, and Chaos
Secrets, Suspicions, and Silence
Revenge, Rescue, and Revelations
Kidnappers, Killers, and Karma
Presents, Poison, and Peril
Hitmen, Hunches, and Havoc - Part 1
Hitmen, Hunches, and Havoc - Part 2

Watch for more at https://books2read.com/ap/81Do3O/
Travis-Cramer.

About the Author

Travis Cramer is a 18-year-old storyteller with roots in the lively state of New Jersey. At 12, his family traded the hustle and bustle for the quieter charm of Delaware—a shift that left young Travis searching for adventure. With fewer distractions in his new surroundings, he turned to his love of fiction as an outlet for creativity. What started as a simple hobby soon transformed into a mission: to write a full-fledged story, beginning to end. From this spark of inspiration, *Misadventure and Mystery* was born—a series where imagination knows no bounds, and every page brims with excitement and intrigue.

Read more at https://books2read.com/ap/81Do3O/Travis-Cramer.